K-9

ROHAN GAVIN

Bloomsbury Publishing, London, New Delhi, New York and Sydney

First published in Great Britain in August 2014 by Bloomsbury Publishing Plc
50 Bedford Square, London WC1B 3DP

www.bloomsbury.com
www.knightleyandson.com

Bloomsbury is a registered trademark of Bloomsbury Publishing Plc

Text copyright © Rohan Gavin 2014
Illustrations copyright © Leo Hartas 2014

The moral rights of the author and illustrator have been asserted

A CIP catalogue record for this book is available from the British Library

ISBN 978 1 4088 5143 2

MIX
Paper from
responsible sources
FSC® C020471
www.fsc.org

Typeset by Hewer Text UK Ltd, Edinburgh
Printed and bound in Great Britain by CPI Group (UK) Ltd, Croydon CR0 4YY

1 3 5 7 9 10 8 6 4 2

For the war dogs

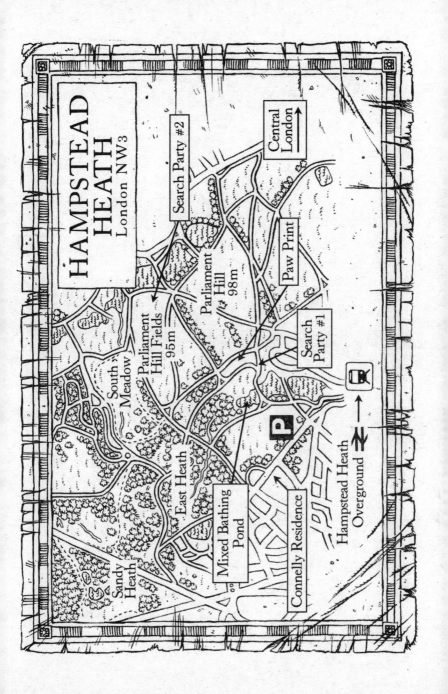

Prologue
NO EXIT

It was a two packet of digestives problem. Possibly even three. And tonight of course he'd only brought a single Club biscuit, which he'd consumed over fifteen minutes ago. The new diet was doing little for his generous waistline and even less for his powers of concentration.

Uncle Bill (also known as Montague Billoch from the Department of the Unexplained) rummaged around in the depths of his coat pockets for any morsel that might have eluded him, finding only one woollen glove, coated in breadcrumbs and lacking a significant other. He gave up, rubbed his hands together against the cold, blew a plume of smoke from the cigar between his teeth and continued his lumbering stride along the brightly lit Victoria Embankment, with the River Thames glittering darkly below.

And still his search had produced nothing: no evidence of the rumoured subterranean tunnels that led from the villains' secret bunker under Down Street Tube station, delivering would-be escapees to the river. No mysterious arches, no doorways in walls. Bill leaned over the stone balustrade, looking down towards the water, finding no footprints in the silty mudflats and no secret moorings where speedboats might have lain in wait. There were no clues whatsoever. He'd begun to think this routine was exactly that: routine. He was also starting to question the wisdom of his long-time colleague and pal, private eye Alan Knightley, who had suggested this fool's errand in the first place. *If* Alan's college-chum-turned-mortal-enemy, Morton Underwood, had somehow escaped from the Tube tracks three months ago, it was anyone's guess where he was now. Also missing were Underwood's colleagues from the sinister crime organisation known as the Combination: an awesome foe that had cast a long shadow over London with its almost supernatural feats of evil and corruption.

The one consolation was that if Alan's thirteen-year-old son, Darkus Knightley, was half as capable a detective as he'd proved on his first case, he would no doubt be following his own lines of inquiry. With the help of that unusual stepsister, Tilly, of course, who wanted to find the Combination for her own reasons: to avenge her mother's death.

Uncle Bill set aside these thoughts and ambled on

past the Houses of Parliament, which were wrapped in a treacly mist, their facets tinted orange by the floodlights. As he walked under the street lamps of Parliament Square, his massive form – with the homburg hat at its apex – cast its own near-planetary shadow over the surroundings. As if on cue, Big Ben began striking midnight, reverberating into the heavens and beyond.

Bill proceeded through the square, navigated two pedestrian crossings and found himself back on the river walk, which was by now deserted. A few passing lorries and minicabs were the only signs of life. Those, and the enormous London Eye watching silently and ominously from the other side of the restless waters.

Bill raised his collar and pressed on, feeling a twinge in his knee from the nasty spill he'd suffered on the Knightleys' last investigation. Hopefully any future cases would be less physically taxing. And less taxing on the already stretched finances of his little-known and little-thought-of department of Scotland Yard. Bill reminded himself that by the time he reached the Millennium Bridge he could, in good conscience, hail a cab, return to his modest but comfortable apartment in Putney and gain access to his secret refreshment cupboard.

As Bill relished this idea he heard a loud click on the pavement behind him. It sounded metallic, like a steel nail falling on to the paving stones with a single strike.

But when he turned around, there was nothing there. Just the dim globes of the street lights, and the trunks of the trees extending evenly into the distance.

Uncle Bill hesitantly removed the cigar from his teeth, examined the scene once more, then continued along the river walk with a slightly more urgent stride. His waddling shadow would have been shambolic were it not for its surprising speed. Bill glanced at the road running alongside him, but of course at this moment, there were no vehicles in sight. Before he could open his mouth to curse, the click returned again – clear as day – like a heavy pin dropping.

This time, Bill spun round with incredible stealth, hoping to catch the culprit in the act.

'Aye mah auntie. Ye ol' bampot,' he blurted in his almost unbelievably thick Scottish accent.

There was still nothing there. Except for . . . a small pair of twinkling eyes approximately fifty metres in his wake. The eyes hovered about a metre off the ground, then they darted back behind a tree.

'Whit? Ya mad dafty . . .'

Bill turned back, trying to act casual, and ambled faster, puffing smoke into the sky. And as the mists parted for a moment, he could make out a perfectly *full moon*.

'Just mah luck –'

At that moment, he was interrupted by a howl so loud that he initially mistook it for a boating horn somewhere on the Thames. But instead of a flat monotone, this sound rose into a feral wail that sent the hair on Bill's back (and there was a generous amount of it) standing on end. And from the guttural rattle of the beast, it sounded even hungrier than Bill was.

Bill took to his heels – which in this case were a pair of orthopaedic loafers that were designed for comfort and support, not for running – and he hurtled head-long down the centre of the river walk, under the light of the moon.

Behind him, the metallic click on the pavement became a clatter as the sharp claws of the beast acceler-ated to a gallop, its eyes unblinking, focused on its prey.

Bill waved his arms at a passing car but the driver failed to notice him through the row of tree trunks – or failed to care. The London Eye continued to watch indifferently from across the river.

The metallic clatter raced up behind Bill, and knowing he had no chance of outrunning it, he turned to face the enemy, his arms spread wide as if he intended to hug it to death.

'Whit da –?'

There was nothing there. Just the dim arc of the street lamp capturing an empty stretch of river walk. Bill blew out his cheeks with relief and took a hefty tug on his cigar. Then, as he turned back around he discovered a low, muscular shape blocking his way, vapour trails rising from its nostrils. Its formidable torso was draped in shadow.

It was a *dog* of some kind. Or a wolf.

The animal's jaws opened as if in slow motion, with half a dozen glistening strings of saliva stretching between the lower mandible and the upper maxilla bone. Like a slippery and lethal musical instrument. Its body was pitch black but its coat shone with youth and vitality, even through the darkness. Its anatomy was ripped with long muscles that Bill couldn't even identify.

Its jaws opened wider, and its thin black lips rolled back to reveal two long rows of perfectly symmetrical and impossibly sharp teeth.

Instead of a howl, the animal emitted a series of rhythmic grunts as if it was delivering some sort of funeral eulogy.

Bill puffed up his chest in a primitive fight-or-flight response. Plumes of smoke escaped his cheeks as he tore the cigar from his mouth and waved its dim ember in the direction of the beast to ward it off. Needless to say, it had profoundly little effect.

'Hing aff us!' he warned, before tossing the cigar over his shoulder, sensing that it would be of no further use.

6

Bill desperately searched his deep coat pockets for any weapon or talisman to save him. Incredibly, his fingers detected the corner of what felt like a torn chocolate wrapper: a rogue Penguin biscuit if he was not mistaken.

Maintaining a poker face, Bill eased the half-eaten biscuit into his grasp – and for a fleeting millisecond he did in fact consider eating it, but then he thought better of it – and quickly yanked it out of his pocket and threw it in the opposite direction. The canine's instincts were confused for a split second as its eyes followed the treat, and Bill darted around the beast, using a tree trunk for cover.

'Ha!' Bill managed as he cantered further down the river walk. He may be a goner, but at least he wasn't going down without a fight.

The metallic clattering of the creature's claws started up with a vengeance, accompanied by an amused growl, indicating the prize would be all the more sweet for this minor setback.

Bill's hat blew off as he ran his version of an Olympic sprint. The slingshot shape of the Millennium Bridge loomed ahead of him, stretching over the water. It was always the end goal, and now Bill sensed it was a matter of life or death. As his orthopaedic loafers covered the distance, the sudden aerobic exercise had the odd side effect of clearing his mind.

Who could have set this beast on him? No idea. Bill had enemies, but he was more bureaucrat than field agent. How could it have tracked him? By smell of course. Something Bill had in plentiful supply. *Smell*. Smell was what he had to rid himself of. And fast.

Bill reached the entrance to the bridge and ran up the walkway, his chest heaving and his overcoat flapping in the wind. The curved railings and lateral suspension beams extended on either side of him with the water bubbling menacingly below.

He managed to get fifty metres across the bridge when he felt the warm breath of the beast on the back of his meaty calves. He turned to face the enemy once more.

The dog was almost smiling, its slick coat glowing in the mist. Playtime was over, it was dinner time now – and Bill presented a buffet spread of possibilities.

'A'right, beastie,' he wheezed.

The dog hissed through its bared teeth.

'Cheerio for nou –' Bill grabbed hold of the railing and hoisted himself over, teetering on the edge for a few seconds, like a side of beef on a butcher's scale.

The dog leaped up at him and bit, tearing away a piece of calf flesh and corduroy. But gravity was on Bill's side, and with another small budge, his full bulk toppled over the edge of the railings.

Somehow, Bill had the forethought to tuck his knees against his belly (as close as his physique would permit) then wrapped his arms around them, forming a human cannonball as he hit the freezing surface of the Thames, ejecting a tower of water into the air in his wake. A bystander on dry land described the scene as similar to a small car being dropped into a lake.

Bill instantly vanished underwater, his entire form being swallowed up by the river. Within moments, the tower of water evaporated and the Thames returned to its restless flow, leaving no trace of him.

The dog watched from the bridge, whined with abject disappointment, then trotted back across the walkway and into the night.

Chapter 1
HEALTHY COMPETITION

Darkus Knightley knelt down in the grass, planting his fingers along the chalk line. Six other runners were positioned alongside him, with the Cranston School sports field extending ahead of them. Although Darkus was physically fit, his frame was slighter than many of his classmates. He considered his physical form a vessel for his brain rather than a tool in itself – although he had, on occasion, needed to rely on it for self-defence. But even then, his brain was the real weapon; his body merely followed orders. He was also far more comfortable in a nicely cut tweed suit than in his own skin – which was currently exposed to the elements with only a running vest, shorts and a clunky pair of trainers for protection. And no hat.

The benefit of exercise, in his mind, was that it dulled the noise of the 'catastrophiser' – that trusty tool of his, which continually digested potential clues from his immediate surroundings and churned out the worst-case scenario. Of course the worst-case scenario was often *not* the case, but when it *was*, the device would quickly unearth the dark, unpalatable truth.

He also found that physical exercise provided a fresh burst of oxygen to help him solve any outstanding cases or logic problems; but, if he was honest, he had precious few of those to solve at the moment, due to the fact that his father, Alan Knightley, had once again disappeared into his work, leaving Darkus behind to deal with the trivial pursuits of school life.

Burke, the sports master, fired the starting pistol, which snapped Darkus's mind into sharp focus. His fingers left the chalk line and balled into fists as his legs projected him down the track. The fifteen hundred metres was a chess game as much as a race and he would need to time it perfectly if he had any hope of finishing in a reasonable position. There was no audience in attendance, and no possibility he could win, but Darkus took a certain pride in everything he did. Strangely, the last time he'd run with such determination was when he was being pursued by Burke the sports master himself. Darkus had assisted his stepsister Tilly with her great escape from the school grounds only three months earlier. Fortunately, Burke had never made a positive identification. Of course back then the stakes had been infinitely higher: saving his father's life; and protecting the world from his one-time godfather Morton Underwood and the evil Combination. Today was a far simpler game.

Matt Wilson, the school champion and an honest competitor, was already moving towards the inside lane, leading the pack. Brendan Doyle, who was built like an outhouse and wasn't exactly charitable by nature – due to an unhappy home life, Darkus deduced – jostled for position, still wearing the hoodie that he routinely used to intimidate fellow classmates. The teachers had put Doyle down a couple of years, which only added to his physical superiority. Darkus allowed Doyle to move in front of him and watched as the bully elbowed other runners out of the way.

Darkus turned the first corner, near the back of the pack – then saw something in the undergrowth at the edge of the track: it was the glint of a single lens. By the diameter of the reflection Darkus estimated it was a telephoto lens, with a focal length of between two hundred and three hundred millimetres. Darkus's catastrophiser started whirring feverishly, stealing oxygen from the rest of his body and raising his heart rate. It was unlikely to be a sniper. There were more discreet ways to dispose of a detective than on a school playing field. But if not, then who was it? As his arms and legs kept moving, his breathing sped up and he experienced a burning sensation in his lungs from gulping down the cold air. As usual, he didn't want to listen to the catastrophiser, but his rational brain provided no reasonable explanation.

Darkus took evasive action by moving forward through the pack to obscure himself from whoever was watching. He saw Doyle in front of him, his hoodie visibly lagging from the exertion. Darkus moved to over-take him.

'What are you doing, *Dorkus?*' the boy demanded.

'Nothing special,' Darkus answered in between breaths.

'Think you're going to beat me or something?'

'Highly unlikely. You have a clear, physical advantage.'

'Then why are you all up in my stuff?'

'Just avoiding someone,' Darkus answered, glancing back to see the glint at six o' clock relative to his current position.

Doyle cocked his hoodie, baffled. 'By the way, it's Friday. What happened to that homework you owe me?'

'I'm afraid I had to go back on our agreement,' Darkus began. 'My hope was that a few good marks would boost your morale and improve your overall performance. But I can see my intervention has had the opposite effect,' he said, catching his breath. 'Might I suggest focusing on sport? Perhaps of the full contact variety?'

Darkus stopped talking, steadied his breathing and continued to move through the pack until he felt a sharp pain in his right thigh. At the same time his right leg buckled and collapsed. He silently tumbled to the grass at the side of the track, feeling a numb, wet sensation on the upper part of his leg. The three other runners in close proximity collided painfully with him and fell nearby. Wilson the school champion slowed down, looking over his shoulder to check that none of his classmates were injured. Doyle accelerated past the leader triumphantly.

Darkus investigated the pain, reaching down to discover a small puncture wound in his thigh, which was oozing blood. The wound was too small for a sniper's bullet, too messy for a knife blade, but perfectly corresponded to a homemade 'shiv' – or improvised blade. Darkus looked up to see Doyle toss just such a weapon – a sharpened plastic comb whose teeth had been removed – into the undergrowth at the edge of the track. Doyle, who was now leading the pack, turned and shot Darkus a sinister smile from under his hoodie.

Darkus ignored this petty assault, and searched instead for the glinting lens, which had now vanished altogether. As Darkus scanned the surroundings, Burke jogged over to him, to inspect the wound.

'You're bleeding, Knightley.' Burke peered over his handlebar moustache.

'Must've caught it on a spike, sir. No harm done.'

Darkus got to his feet, took out a monogrammed handkerchief, bound up his leg, and completed the race.

He came last.

Darkus's mum, Jackie, was waiting at the school gates with Wilburforce sitting obediently beside her, his bat-ears twitching at every small sound. When Darkus approached in his usual tweed jacket and waistcoat ensemble, Wilbur wagged his tail once, which was normally the extent of the greeting. Darkus wasn't offended by this, because he knew the German shepherd was still recovering from the deafeningly loud noises he'd encountered during his long career in the K-9 unit of the bomb disposal squad. Darkus didn't know all the case histories because they were classified, but he could see by the greying temples and the tired eyes that Wilbur had seen more than most dogs (or people) would ever wish to.

Wilbur had been a gift from Darkus's father, Alan, after their first assignment. It was fair to say that this recent addition to the family hadn't gone down brilliantly with Darkus's stepdad, Clive. It had only been a matter of months since Clive suffered under the hypnotic powers of the villain Morton Underwood and had an embarrassing on-air meltdown while filming his TV series, *Wheel Spin* – which was then taken off the air. And now an emotionally fragile police dog had moved into his house, leaving unexplained puddles (or worse) in the garage and sitting in his favourite La-Z-Boy chair. For some reason, Wilbur's post-traumatic stress disorder only ever seemed to affect Clive's belongings. Darkus, Jackie, and Clive's daughter, Tilly, were all immune. Their clothes never went missing and their things were never chewed or found their way to the bottom of the garden. Clive, however, was fair game for all of Wilbur's less sociable habits and there was no end to the missing gloves, hats, boxer shorts and DVDs that he would complain to Jackie about.

Darkus and Jackie talked in private about the fact that Clive's mind hadn't been the same since his own trauma – and he seemed to routinely forget where he'd put things. So perhaps the objects that were going missing weren't *all* Wilbur's fault. Naturally, Clive was convinced that the *Schweinhund* (German for pig-dog) was responsible for everything that was wrong in the house. Jackie had relented and tried a local dog trainer, with no success. After that she hired a 'dog whisperer', but the words fell on deaf ears. Next, Jackie tried an even more alternative therapy and visited a friend of a friend who specialised in natural remedies, including herbal extracts and flower essences. Wilbur tried taking what was known as a 'rescue remedy' with his morning meal, but the only discernible effect was that he trotted around the house for the rest of the day with his tail between his legs, peeing uncontrollably.

'How was school?' enquired Jackie, bringing Darkus back to the present.

'The usual,' Darkus replied, then put on his tweed walking hat and patted Wilbur on the head. 'Attaboy,' he whispered.

Wilbur wrinkled his jowls and lifted his whiskers in a half-smile.

Doyle appeared through the school gates, tightening the strings of his hoodie and flashing a gang sign of some kind at Darkus, who smiled and waved by way of reply. Wilbur growled protectively, straining on the lead.

'Easy . . .' Darkus reassured the mutt. 'Nothing I can't handle.'

Tilly appeared through the gates next, in a leather jacket with her hair in purple dip-dyed pigtails. 'What up, fam?'

'We're fine, thank you, Tilly,' said Jackie, and led the motley-looking group towards their waiting estate car.

Darkus tapped his stepsister on the shoulder, leaving Jackie to put Wilbur in the back of the car. 'Don't take

17

this the wrong way, but were you watching me on the playing field?' he asked.

'Me?' Tilly snipped. 'No. Why would I be doing that?'

Despite the easing of relations on their first case, Darkus was reminded that Tilly's default setting would always be defensive since losing her mother, Carol – who'd been Darkus's father's assistant.

'Never mind,' he said, puzzled.

At that moment, a blonde female classmate darted out of the school gates and approached them. Tilly instinctively moved to block her: 'Can I help you?'

'My name's Alexis,' the blonde introduced herself. 'Friends call me Lex.'

'I know who you are,' said Tilly disdainfully, giving her the once-over. 'Editor-in-chief of *The Cranston Star*.'

'And chief photographer,' added Darkus, who couldn't help observing Alexis's slender legs, against which a long-lensed camera dangled from a strap over her shoulder. She was a year older than him, but at this age, it felt like an aeon.

'Guilty as charged,' replied Alexis, her lips curling into a cockeyed smile. She plucked a small twig from her blonde tresses, then flicked it away.

'You were watching me on the playing field,' deduced Darkus.

'Sorry if I distracted you,' she answered.

Tilly looked from Alexis to Darkus, unsure if she was detecting chemistry.

'If you wanted a photo, you only needed to ask,' said Darkus and shrugged on his herringbone overcoat.

'I wasn't after a glamour shot, Darkus. Or should I say . . . "Doc". The truth is, I'm breaking a story.'

'Really?' Tilly interjected. 'And what's the subject matter?'

'It's autobiographical, really. You see, I was on the Piccadilly Line last October, over half-term. Dad was taking me to a matinee . . .' she said coyly. 'I don't remember what film to be honest.'

'So?' demanded Tilly. 'For a journalist you certainly take a long time getting to the point.'

'I witnessed a unique air pressure phenomenon while we were underground,' said Alexis flatly. 'A freak tornado. You may've heard about it?'

Tilly and Darkus glanced at each other, realising that what she had actually witnessed was their climactic battle with the Combination.

'You must have been seeing things,' Darkus answered.

'Well, that's the funny thing,' said Alexis. 'What I was seeing was *you*, Darkus.'

'A reflection of one of the other passengers perhaps,' he countered. 'A trick of the light.'

19

Tilly remained quiet.

Alexis continued: 'The person I saw was around thirteen years old, standing on a disused Tube platform, wearing a tweed hat, and a herringbone overcoat. He was accompanied by a scrawny-looking female around the same age.'

'What d'you mean, "scrawny"?' snapped Tilly, then fell silent, before trying for a save. 'I mean . . . Tube lines run at over fifty miles per hour so it must've been hard to tell.'

'Oh, she was scrawny, all right,' Alexis confirmed, as Tilly's heavily mascaraed eyes went wide. Alexis turned to Darkus. 'Is it true your father was the renowned London detective . . . Alan Knightley?'

'Not was. *Is*,' Darkus responded, even though he hadn't heard from his dad in almost a month, and had no idea what he was currently working on. His father had clearly forgotten the success of their first investigation and was now operating on his own – although Darkus wasn't convinced his dad's reasoning powers were up to the job. His dad had recovered from the four-year-long coma inflicted on him by Underwood, but had proved he was still liable to return to that unconscious state at the drop of a tweed hat. In the absence of any clues as to what Knightley was *really* doing, Darkus could only speculate.

Alexis continued her line of questioning: 'Then I suppose it's not too big a stretch to assume your father might have been investigating something on the tracks?'

'Kids?' Jackie called over from the car. Wilbur whimpered as the boot was closed.

'I don't comment on my father's work,' said Darkus. Tilly grabbed him by the coat sleeve and dragged him towards the car. 'Now, if you'll excuse us, Lex,' Darkus said over his shoulder, 'we're late for tea. Have a pleasant weekend.'

Tilly muttered to herself as she slung her rucksack in the back seat and got in. '*Lex* . . . I mean, who can take someone with a name like that seriously?'

'She certainly has a very analytical mind,' Darkus commented as he got in the front.

'Analytical my –' Tilly slammed the door and Jackie accelerated away.

Chapter 2
A TEMPOROSPATIAL PROBLEM

When they got home to their mock-Tudor house on Wolseley Close they found the Jaguar coupe parked half off the driveway, splattered with bird sap and looking distinctly less cared for than it used to. Its owner, Jackie's husband, Clive, sat in the living room in his favourite chair, engrossed in an episode of an Australian soap opera.

'Hello, sweetie –' Jackie ventured.

Clive snapped his fingers loudly to signal absolute silence. Tilly shook her head in dismay and went up to her room. Wilbur duly walked around the sofa, blocking Clive's view of the TV, then wagged his tail, knocking a vase off a side table.

'That hound from hell – !' Clive exclaimed. '*Raus!! Schnell!*' he cried out in German, for no apparent reason.

Wilbur slouched into a hunting position, then crawled under the sofa and started clawing at something beneath.

'*Nein!!* Watch the parquet flooring! For crying out loud . . .'

Wilbur reappeared with his favourite chew toy in his mouth: a rubber Kong with a black and white chequered band – symbol of the Metropolitan Police.

'Give – !' Clive wrestled Wilbur for the toy, also for no apparent reason. Then his phone rang and he dug in the front pocket of his nylon shell suit and answered it. 'Yes . . . ?' Clive spun to face Darkus and Jackie. '*Shhhhhhhh!* It's my agent.'

'We didn't say anything, darling,' whispered Jackie.

'Zippit! No, Veronique, not you, luvvie,' he warbled. 'Shoot . . .' Clive continued grappling with the dog toy, having forgotten why he was playing with it in the first place. He listened for several seconds, his face dropping under the force of gravity. 'A reality show? In Albania? Well, what's it paying? OK. OK. OK. *Ciao.*'

'Everything OK, darling?' Jackie enquired.

'Bloody awful as a matter of fact,' Clive grumbled. 'Ever since this beast arrived in our home, my luck's gone from bad to terrible –' He tore the chew toy away from Wilbur and waved it around, spraying himself with dog slobber, although he didn't appear to notice.

'Darling?' Jackie interjected.

'Let me finish!' Clive barked, then waved the saliva-soaked toy around again, proclaiming: 'I could've been a contender . . . Maybe even the host of my own panel show. Now I can't get on telly anywhere in the developed world. And *this* . . . this odorous furball.' Clive dangled the toy over Wilbur's snout. 'My one consolation is the fact that Alan obviously couldn't afford a real dog. And fortunately, this one looks like it's only a few good walks from the pet cemetery –'

'Clive!' Jackie snapped.

'Well, it's true.'

Darkus winced, but he had to admit that, like everything he received from his father, Wilbur was unusual and to some degree damaged. But that didn't make Darkus love Wilbur any less; in fact it made him love the dog more.

'Come on, boy,' said Darkus, but Wilbur remained hypnotised by Clive's offer of the toy.

'Want to play, do you?' Clive told the mutt, then got to his feet and stalked to the front door. With one quick motion Clive ran out on to the driveway and hurled the toy across the road and into a nearby field. 'Go fetch!'

Darkus watched in horror as Wilbur shot through the open doorway and galloped into the road – straight into the path of an oncoming car.

24

'Wilbur!' Darkus cried out.

Wilbur stood frozen on the spot as the motorist slammed on the brakes and skidded towards him. Then at the last possible moment the dog yelped and swerved out of the way, hopping over the fence into the neighbouring plot.

Darkus raced out into the road after him.

'Doc! Watch out!' Jackie called after him, as he ran in front of the motorist who was still at a halt in the middle of the road, looking left and right, waiting for his path to clear.

'Wilbur!' Darkus continued to yell, but the German shepherd was now deep in the tall grass of the overgrown field.

Darkus took hold of the fence and climbed over it, tearing the hem of his overcoat without a second glance. He entered the tall grass after his dog.

'Here, boy . . .' he called out, but only got a distant whimper in return.

The grass moved ten metres in front of him but he still couldn't see Wilbur.

'It's OK, boy. Come home,' he said softly, but loud enough for the dog to hear.

The grass continued to move further and further away from him, until he saw Wilbur's bat-ears appear on a small bluff in the centre of the field. He had the chew toy in his mouth but wouldn't budge.

'Come home!' Darkus called to him. Wilbur whined and shook his head, waving the toy. 'It'll be OK, I promise,' he pleaded, but Wilbur's ears vanished into the grass again, retreating further into the field.

Tilly watched the scene unfold from her bedroom window, sadly.

Darkus waded over to the bluff, climbed up it and spotted the dog lying in the grass some way off. Darkus knelt down, reached in his pocket and fished out the secure phone that Uncle Bill had given him on their last investigation. Then he fished out the stainless-steel business-card holder his father had given him, and flipped it open to reveal the stack of cards lying untouched inside, all displaying the words: *Knightley & Son*. He turned the top card over to find the small, embossed symbol of the 'evil eye': a symbol of protection as well as fear. Darkus dialled the 0845 number on the front of the card and waited while the line rang. There was a short pause as the call was redirected, then after a few moments, his father's Polish housekeeper picked up.

'Knightley's Investigations? This is Bogna in Admins?' she answered in her broken English.

'Bogna, it's Darkus.'

'Doc! Is everything OK?'

'Where's Dad?'

'On assignments. He not tell me what.'

'But he's OK?' enquired Darkus. 'No more "episodes"?'

'You mean unconscious coma state? No, nothing like that.'

'I see . . .'

Darkus furrowed his brow. Not only was his father not available, he was on a case that he hadn't bothered to share with him – his son, heir, and most importantly his partner. Darkus's deepest suspicions were proved right: the partnership with his dad was for demonstration purposes only; it was merely a way to pacify Darkus, rather than the genuine article. After waking from his coma, his father had accepted his help, made the promises, printed the business cards, but in reality Darkus was as in the dark as he'd ever been.

'When d'you expect him back?' asked Darkus.

'You know Alan. Could be any times.'

'OK, thanks, Bogna. Please let him know I called.'

'Affirmatives, Master Doc.'

In the kitchen, Jackie and Clive were engaged in a Mexican stand-off. Jackie poured hot water over a teabag, then slid the mug across the counter towards Clive with the ferocity of a bartender in a Wild West saloon.

'He loves that dog,' she said accusingly.

27

'Not my fault it nearly got itself killed,' Clive replied meekly.

'He doesn't love many things, Clive. Not after losing Alan for all those years.'

'Again . . . not my fault if his dad's a nutjob with a tendency to fall into strange, coma-like trances. And now the man's awake, he's not exactly the most attentive father. They may talk the same and dress the same, but Alan hasn't been round in months.' Clive dumped the teabag in the sink and splashed the milk in.

'Life hasn't dealt Doc the easiest of hands, but I want him to be able to love. And to trust again. Do you understand me, Clive?' He didn't answer. 'Do you . . . ?' Jackie trailed off, seeing her son standing in the doorway, without Wilbur.

'He won't come home,' said Darkus, pretending that he hadn't just overheard the conversation. 'He won't listen to me.'

'Give it time, sweetie,' Jackie consoled him. 'How about a jam sandwich? Triangles not squares?'

Darkus couldn't raise a smile; instead he glanced through the kitchen window to see dusk falling and the field sinking into foreboding shadow.

Behind him, Clive started patting down his shell suit, searching for something. 'Now, where's my ruddy phone?' He tried several zipped pockets but none bore fruit. He slammed his mug down on the table and pushed back his chair. 'Right! That. Is. It. The hellhound has eaten it.'

'I'm afraid there's a temporospatial problem with your statement, Clive,' Darkus suggested.

'Come again?' said his stepdad.

'You were speaking on the phone only moments before you threw the toy across the road. Wilbur couldn't have had time to take your phone before running across the road.'

'Doc's right,' agreed Jackie.

'And I suppose you think it just –' Clive made a mushroom cloud gesture – 'vanished into thin air?'

They were interrupted by a light rap on the kitchen door. Darkus darted over and opened it to reveal Wilbur sitting there with his paw raised. The chew toy was lying discarded by his side, and balanced in his mouth was a small handset in a dayglo orange case, which Darkus instantly recognised as his stepfather's phone.

'Ha!' accused Clive. 'The truth is out!' He marched forward and yanked the phone from Wilbur's mouth. 'Well, my furry nemesis . . .'

'Er, Clive?' Darkus interjected.

'What is it now?' he hissed.

'If you examine the handset you'll see there are no signs of chewing. A good deal of saliva, I'll warrant.

But no bite marks,' Darkus pointed out. Clive turned the sticky phone over in his hand as he listened. 'Instead you'll find a small clod of loose earth embedded in the edge of the case, which is consistent with the fact that when you threw the chew toy into the field, you also dispatched your mobile phone at the same time.' Darkus stated it plainly for him: 'You threw them *both*.'

Clive unconsciously dropped the phone on the floor, and his eyebrows arched with fury.

'Wilbur didn't take your phone,' Darkus concluded. 'In fact, he returned it to you.'

'Prove it!' Clive yapped.

'I just did,' Darkus replied.

'Not well enough,' declared his stepdad and lunged at Wilbur, who dodged round him and headed off into the living room. 'Come back here, you infernal beast!'

'Clive, really . . .' Jackie reasoned.

Wilbur sat patiently, confused, on the Persian rug. Clive stared him down from the doorway of the kitchen. Darkus walked over to console the dog, until a sudden bang, like a gunshot, echoed from the street outside. Wilbur jumped, then froze on the spot.

'It's OK, boy, it's only a car backfiring,' Darkus deduced, then noticed a small, yellow puddle forming under Wilbur's back legs. 'Oh no . . .'

The puddle rapidly spread out, forming a large, golden circle, penetrating the carpet fibres and soaking into the Persian rug.

'Oh, now you've done it . . .' Clive murmured. 'That rug has been in the Palmer family since the Battle of Khartoum!' He jabbed his hand towards the ceiling. 'Out!'

Clive stormed towards the dog until Wilbur's lips rolled back and he snarled dangerously, displaying both rows of teeth.

Clive reared up and retreated, turning to Jackie for support. 'That dog,' he stammered, 'is to be out of this house by noon tomorrow. Or I'm checking into the Premier Inn. *Permanently*.' Clive stamped his Adidas slip-on sandal emphatically. 'It's him or me.'

Darkus knew who he'd prefer, but, in spite of everything, his mother would remain loyal to the man she'd married.

Darkus went to Wilbur's side, but recoiled when the German shepherd flinched, snarled in his direction and barked twice – shocking Darkus who fell back on his elbows. Then the dog turned tail and ran back through the kitchen door, towards the shed.

Darkus looked to his mother with tears welling up in his eyes. 'It's not his fault.'

'It's for the best, darling,' she replied softly. 'It just hasn't . . . worked out.'

'It's not fair,' Darkus whispered defiantly.

Jackie went to hug him, but Darkus shrugged her off then turned and followed Wilbur through the back door into the falling darkness. Jackie watched him go, looking like a piece of her heart had been torn out.

Wilbur sat in the corner of the garden, forlorn, then wagged his tail once as Darkus cautiously went to join him. Wilbur's ears were flat against his head; his brow furrowed as if to say he was truly sorry. Darkus slowly extended his hand and patted him. Wilbur wagged his tail once more.

'What are we going to do?' Darkus whispered to him.

Wilbur looked up at him with tired grey eyes, unable to provide any answers.

'I'll come and visit you,' said Darkus, feeling his own eyes well up again. He knew it wasn't entirely rational, but he couldn't help it. Since his father had effectively disappeared for the second time, Wilbur was the only person he really talked to. Not that Wilbur was equipped to give him any advice, but Darkus found he could have better conversations with him, and discover more about himself, than he could by talking to anyone else.

As they sat on the grass they both felt the chill creep in. They could hear Clive talking to the TV while Jackie did the washing-up – routinely checking on Darkus through the kitchen window. Darkus waited as long as possible, then got to his feet. Wilbur dutifully followed his master through the back door into the house. Jackie handed Darkus a plate of jam sandwiches, which he carried upstairs with Wilbur in tow.

In the privacy of his bedroom, Darkus gave his dog a triangle, then took one for himself. Wilbur consumed his in one bite, then looked up at his master, pleading for another. Darkus obliged, then went to his desk, took out the secure phone and scrolled to the name: *Uncle Bill*. Seeing Wilbur begging, Darkus gave him another two triangles, then pressed 'Dial'.

After two rings, a thick Scottish voice answered: 'Aye?'

'Uncle Bill? It's Darkus here.'

'A'right, Darkus. Only it's *nae* Uncle Bill. This is his brother, *Dougal*. Ah'm afraid Bill is currently . . . indisposed.'

Darkus looked at the phone, surprised: the similarity in their Highland accents was uncanny. He'd heard talk of Dougal, who operated a lighthouse in the Outer Hebrides, but why would he be answering Bill's private line?

'Is everything OK?' said Darkus.

'Well, nae exactly, nay,' replied Dougal in the negative. 'I cannae say much, but Bill has been admitted tae

33

hospital again, this time with quite serious injuries. Our mam insisted I come doon tae have a swatch.'

If the family were keeping a vigil, it had to be serious. 'What kind of injuries? What happened?'

'Ah'm sorry, Darkus, but I cannae say. Bill's expected to pull throoough but he's under twintie-four-hoor police guard. The rest is classified *top secret*.'

Darkus's mind left his own domestic problems and began turning the facts over in his head. His father had gone off the radar. Bill was in hospital. Something was most definitely afoot. He realised he couldn't press Dougal any further.

'Kindly send Bill a packet of chocolate digestives from me. And have him call me as soon as he's well enough.'

'Will dae,' replied Dougal.

Darkus hung up, his mind racing but having insufficient data to get anywhere.

From downstairs came the sound of Jackie and Clive engaged in a heated discussion.

Darkus told Wilbur: 'Wait.' Then he crept out of his bedroom, across the landing and halfway down the stairs.

'. . . now if we hired someone like *her*, it might be a different story,' Clive pointed out.

An image glimmered on the TV set, showing a hulking, middle-aged woman, dressed in country tweed.

Her bombastic figure appeared to be trussed up inside a tailored hunting outfit and Hunter wellington boots. Her index finger was raised commandingly as she towered over a golden retriever.

'Ssssstay,' the woman on TV instructed the retriever. She then backed away as the dog sat, seemingly terrified, on the spot.

Darkus recognised the woman as Fiona Connelly, star of the popular dog training series *Bad Dog*.

'Well, can't you make some calls?' Jackie asked her husband. 'Try and contact her? I mean, you're "in TV".'

'I may be "in TV", Jax, but I'm not "*on* TV". I've got about as much pull as an . . .'

'Aston Martin?' suggested Jackie cheerily.

'Austin Metro,' Clive replied grimly.

The TV switched to the evening news. A female reporter stood in a dark London street, speaking to camera: 'More reports this evening of aggressive dogs attacking innocent civilians, with devastating results. The government is announcing new tighter controls on dog ownership –'

'As right they should.' Clive idly flicked to another channel.

Darkus frowned, returning to his bedroom where he found the rest of the jam sandwiches had strangely vanished. Wilbur sat in the corner of the room, looking at the carpet.

'It's OK. I wasn't hungry anyway –'

Wilbur made a small guttural yelp and looked up.

'What is it, boy?'

Wilbur trotted to the bedroom window, reared up and rested his front paws on the sill.

On the street below, Darkus and Wilbur observed a shadow slope across the pavement and arrive under the single lamp post opposite the house. It was a *dog* of some kind. Sinewy and ripped with muscles under its slick, ebony coat. It was too dark and the distance was too great to make out exactly what breed it was.

'What d'you think it wants?' Darkus whispered.

Wilbur whimpered and prepared to bark, until Darkus put a hand over his jaws. 'Wait.'

The dog under the lamp post appeared to turn and inspect Clive and Jackie's house – for a good ten seconds. Then it walked in measured strides along the pavement as a *second* shape appeared from the darkness. It was another *identical* dog, taut and composed. What was even stranger was the two dogs then stood facing each other snout to snout under the lamp post, as if they were conversing with each other. Planning, even.

'What are they *doing* . . . ?' Darkus pondered.

Wilbur whined again, registering the very odd scene that was unfolding below them. Then, as quickly as they'd appeared, the two dogs turned and ran away in opposite directions, leaving only a swirl of mist in their wake.

Chapter 3
HOME FROM HOME

An hour later, Wilbur finally left the window, went to the basket at the end of Darkus's bed, chased his tail and curled up in a ball. Within moments, the dog was asleep.

Darkus buttoned his plaid pyjamas and attempted to follow suit, but was distracted by the distant whine of a motor scooter, which appeared to be approaching Wolseley Close. Wilbur cocked his ears, then ignored it.

The scooter sputtered to a halt outside the house, just as Tilly's bedroom door opened, then closed abruptly and footsteps thumped down the stairs and across the hallway.

Clive shouted something from the master bedroom but the front door slammed before he could finish his sentence.

Darkus got out of bed and returned to his vantage point at the bedroom window, watching as Tilly marched down the driveway to meet the waiting scooter: a gleaming machine finished in red and black. Sitting astride the machine was a young white male in white trainers, grey sweatpants, a puffa jacket and a black carbon helmet sporting what appeared to be devil horns on either side of the visor.

To Darkus's profound puzzlement and mild irritation, Tilly planted a kiss on the cheek of the rider and hopped on the back of the scooter, wrapping her arms around his waist. The rider straightened up, cranked the accelerator and sputtered away with Tilly holding on tight. They turned the corner at the end of the street and the noise reduced to a distant buzz, then vanished altogether.

More perplexed than ever, Darkus left the window and returned to bed.

Darkus slept uncertainly, remaining on the surface of consciousness, never quite reaching a satisfactory depth.

At the edge of his brain, he heard Tilly return home a couple of hours later, accompanied by the brief report of the motor scooter before it buzzed off into the distance.

When morning eventually arrived, Darkus had the momentary illusion that he was waking from a bad dream. But as grey light peered through the curtains, the reality set in – that although he hadn't known Wilbur for long, Darkus was losing the best friend he'd ever had.

Wilbur appeared to be having nightmares of his own, letting out a series of whimpers and crying sounds before raising his head at the end of the bed in a silent greeting. Much as it hurt, Darkus knew that Wilbur would be well cared for, returning to his former home at the dog rescue centre where his dad had first found him. And Darkus would visit as regularly as his schoolwork allowed.

His train of thought was interrupted by Wilbur licking his face.

'Yuk, Wilbur. OK, boy.' Darkus got out of bed and stumbled towards the bathroom.

Downstairs, Tilly was eating a large bowl of cereal with Clive watching in silence from the opposite end of the kitchen table.

'Well . . . ? Who is he?' Clive demanded flatly. 'This mysterious character on the two-wheeled bottle rocket.'

Jackie raised her eyebrows and continued emptying the dishwasher.

'A friend,' Tilly replied.

'*Hmm*,' Clive intoned accusingly.

Wilbur appeared from the staircase and snuck around the outside of the table with his head down, arriving at the dog bowl Jackie had placed by the back door.

'What's wrong with Wilbur?' asked Tilly.

'Holiday's over. He's checking out,' replied Clive, unable to conceal his good spirits. 'Going back to the orphanage, aren't you, boy? *Vorsprung durch Technik*,' he added in his bad German.

Tilly looked at her father in dismay, then shook her head and continued eating her cereal.

'Right. I'm going to get the papers,' Clive announced and jogged lightly to the front door, adjusting his shell suit. 'Back in a mo.'

Tilly and Jackie exchanged a mutually sympathetic glance, then went about their business, until a high-pitched shout interrupted them.

'Jackie!!!' Clive's voice reverberated through the kitchen windows.

'Yes?!'

'The dog's fouled the driveway! Tell Darkus to clean it up.'

'It wasn't Wilbur,' Darkus replied from the kitchen doorway. 'It's obvious from the diameter of the —'

'OK, sweetie. I believe you,' Jackie stopped him.

'There were two other dogs out there last night,' he went on. 'I don't know who they belong to. I've never seen them before.'

'I'm afraid that doesn't change the situation, Doc,' she said gently. 'Wilbur and Clive just aren't compatible.'

41

Darkus looked down, trying to think of a solution to the impending catastrophe, but finding none.

'Look, darling, sometimes you've just got to have a little faith in the world. OK?' Wilbur went to sit by Darkus's side. 'Why don't you two go play in the garden for a while, and I'll put Wilbur's basket in the car.'

The drive to the dog rescue centre took less than an hour, but felt like an eternity. Wilbur was completely silent, yet Darkus felt more attuned to him than ever – as if they were both facing a life sentence to be served in separate cells.

Jackie drove through the tall, metal gates of the compound and saw a well-built fifty-year-old man in grey combat fatigues, waiting for them in the car park. He had the gait of a military officer and clipped, receding hair, which framed a chiselled but kind face with soft blue eyes. From the back seat, Wilbur looked up and wagged his tail once, recognising the figure.

Jackie stepped out of the car while Darkus opened the boot for Wilbur. A few distant barks signalled the presence of the other residents of the rescue centre, which consisted of a nondescript concrete block overlooking a large, fenced recreation yard.

'Captain Reed?' Jackie enquired.

'Call me John.' The man extended his hand. 'Hello, Wilburforce.'

Darkus felt a tug as Wilbur trotted towards his former master and sat obediently by his side.

'I'm really sorry,' Jackie began. 'We just can't keep him any more.'

Darkus said nothing, keeping his hands in the pockets of his herringbone coat, unwilling to make eye contact.

'It doesn't surprise me. I'm sure you did your best,' Reed said diplomatically. 'All of you,' he added, directed at Darkus. Reed ruffled the German shepherd's fur. 'Wilbur's a "war dog". He's seen things most people could never hope to recover from. These dogs, they saved a great many lives – including my own.' Reed stroked the dark patch between Wilbur's ears, losing himself in recollection for a moment. 'In my experience, people let you down. But dogs, they never do.' He looked up, gesturing to the rescue centre. 'This is my way of paying them back.'

'Can I visit him?' Darkus asked, fiddling with his hat.

'It's not up to me,' Reed replied.

Darkus looked down again.

'You'll have to talk to *her* . . .' Reed pointed off towards a classic London black cab parked in a corner at the end of the yard. The driver's door opened and Bogna stepped out in a pair of wrap-around sunglasses, waving cheerfully as she came to greet them.

Darkus broke into a broad smile and turned to his mum. 'You mean . . . ?'

Jackie nodded. 'Wilbur's going to live with Bogna and your dad. You can visit him whenever you like . . . I told you to have a little faith sometimes.'

Darkus spontaneously gave his mum a hug, then knelt down and grabbed Wilbur in an embrace. Wilbur raised his snout proudly, then sniffed at Bogna's brightly coloured housecoat, smelling a variety of strange and powerful odours.

'Hello, Wilburs. You come to live with Bogna now, yes?'

Wilbur wagged once in response.

'Where's Dad?' Darkus asked her.

Bogna shook her head uncertainly. 'I haven't seen much of him in a fort's night.'

'Can I go with them?' Darkus asked his mum.

'If you want,' she said, feeling that same tug herself. 'Just be careful, and be home tomorrow night in time for school.'

'OK, Mum.' Darkus attached the lead to Wilbur's collar and walked him towards his father's black cab without a second glance. Bogna hurried to keep up.

Wilbur stopped, and looked back at Reed for a

moment. The captain called out: 'I'm here if you need me. That goes for both of you.'

Wilbur twitched his ears. Darkus looked back and nodded, then stepped into the back of the cab with the dog, and within a few moments they had accelerated out of the gate, indicating right, but turning left, and vanishing from view.

Jackie winced as she watched them go, then turned to Reed. 'Thank you.'

'It'll take a lot to split those two up,' he replied with a brief nod – almost a salute. A chorus of light yelps from the main building punctuated the moment. 'Now if you'll excuse me, Mrs Palmer, it's nearly time for their walk.'

'Of course.' Jackie returned to her car alone and headed home.

As Bogna swerved and jolted them towards London, Darkus felt like he was introducing Wilbur to a new part of his life – one that had lain dormant for too long. Once Wilbur was fed and settled into his new digs, Darkus intended to track down his father, wherever he might be. His aim was to find out what case he was pursuing – for he was in no doubt his dad was on a case – and to figure out how it related to their injured colleague,

Uncle Bill. If Knightley Senior hadn't been seen regularly for two weeks, then two things were abundantly clear: firstly, the case was consuming his every waking minute; and secondly – due to the fact that the first forty-eight hours (the most important in any investigation) had elapsed – the case was clearly *not* going to plan. Whatever trail his dad was following was likely to be cold, and perhaps Darkus could help to warm it up.

Bogna guided the Fairway black cab through the warren of north London streets with surprising ease, and before long they were entering the borough of Islington and turning the corner into Cherwell Place.

The short, terraced street with the almost imperceptible curve still looked as if it was being observed through a magnifying glass – just as Darkus remembered it. Bogna pulled into the narrow garage in the alley nearby. Then Darkus led Wilbur toward number 27 while Bogna yanked down the garage door and locked it.

As Bogna let them into the house, Darkus already sensed that his father was absent. The frenetic energy of his presence was lacking, and the place felt lonely despite being immaculately well kept.

'OK, Mister Troubles, you're coming with me,' Bogna instructed Wilbur, who obediently followed her into the kitchen. 'I hope you like goulash,' she added.

Satisfied that Wilbur was in good hands, Darkus climbed the stairs to the top floor and crossed the short landing to the heavy oak door with the engraving: *Alan Knightley, BA, MA, Private Investigator.* Darkus slowly turned the handle and entered his father's office. The wood-panelled room was exactly as he remembered it, the shelves weighed down with books, the broad, mahogany desk sitting at the front window with the globe and the slightly dated computer facing the leather office chair.

Darkus approached the desk and ran his hand over the empty chair back, imagining his father in it and divining what he might be working on. The desk was covered in scraps of paper and receipts – mostly for Pizza Express. Not wishing to pry, Darkus surveyed the debris from a distance rather than sorting through it or 'processing the scene' – which would have been too much of a breach of privacy, even though the subject in question was his father. However, in clear sight among the clutter were several train tickets, each with the same words printed on them: *Hampstead Heath.* It was a sprawling urban wilderness located in north London, popular with romantic couples, ramblers and tourists; but what his father wanted with it was a mystery.

Finding nothing more of note, Darkus heeded the call of nature and crossed the landing to the bathroom. He closed the door behind him, then approached the toilet, only to see a book left open on a small table within arm's length of the seat. The book looked to be at least fifty years old, and was tattered and torn, its spine broken and bent. The page it was left open at displayed a large, ink-drawn illustration of a gigantic dog of some kind, its fangs bared, its tail arched and its claws raised in attack. Most noticeable though were its eyes: monstrous, glittering eyes that were the very personification of evil. Darkus visibly recoiled from the image, folded the corner of the page to mark it, then slammed the book closed. It was then that he saw the front cover, and the title, in ancient, Gothic script:

The Anatomy of a Werewolf

Chapter 4
HIS FATHER'S
FOOTSTEPS

Darkus arrived at Hampstead Heath overground train station just after noon and climbed the steps to the exit. He took several minutes to get his bearings, imagining himself to be his father, and seeing the world the way he would have done.

Darkus noted a modest fruit stall, a zebra crossing, several mums pushing prams, a row of shops and a nearby supermarket. To his right was the entrance to Hampstead Heath itself. The huge, ancient park was located on a high ridge overlooking central London. The only guide was a small welcome map displaying an extensive jigsaw of shapes and paths. The eight-hundred-acre wilderness featured dense woodland, numerous parks and meadows, several ponds and a palatial estate called Kenwood House – not to mention the legions of devoted Londoners, joggers, hikers and dog walkers who protected their rural oasis with pride.

According to his research, 'The Heath', as it had become known, dated back well over a thousand years to the reign of King Ethelred the Unready, and was the property of various monarchs and their cronies, before being handed back to the general public in the mid-twentieth century. Beneath the trees, grass and mud lay a band of London clay, a network of underground water-courses and a host of scuttling, burrowing and foraging creatures who also called it home.

Darkus observed his surroundings again and felt his catastrophiser begin to warm up. Much of the time this mental device was a curse that made everything around him part of a dastardly plot, which, admittedly, was often pure fantasy. Until recently that was, when the plots had become reality. For when the catastrophiser was correct – and it was with increasing regularity – it gave Darkus an almost clairvoyant ability to read the signs that were dotted around him. Signs that almost everyone else in the world was blissfully unaware of.

As he glanced past the fruit stall, he remembered his father's particular fondness for satsuma oranges – and his unusual habit of skinning the orange with one small, vertical incision while leaving the rest of the orange peel completely intact. Darkus deduced that one or two of these small oranges would have been too few for a walk like this; four would have been sufficient; but six was a satisfying round number that rolled off the tongue as 'half a dozen'. Therefore, Darkus concluded that his father would almost certainly have bought half a dozen of these small oranges from the fruit stall before embarking any further. This was pure speculation of course. Imagination, even. But imagination was the basis of detective work, until the facts arrived to support it.

Darkus gave a brief description of his father to the fruit seller, who told him he couldn't possibly remember every customer – despite the fact that this particular customer would have been wearing a distinctive Donegal tweed ensemble. Darkus accepted the seller's answer, bought half a dozen oranges and divided them among the pockets of his herringbone coat, then walked up the gentle incline and through the gates on to Hampstead Heath.

He followed a tree-lined path towards the first expanse of grass, which overlooked two ponds, speckled with ducks and the occasional swan. He passed a wooden bench, which had an engraving calligraphed on it:

For Doris. She loved this place. 1910–1995

Other memorial benches were positioned at scenic viewpoints throughout the park.

Darkus observed a few couples strolling along, a

handful of avid joggers, some dogs leading their owners, but nothing more intriguing than that. He walked further, his mind wandering the multitude of footpaths to guess which one his father might have taken. To anyone else, it would have appeared an impossible task. But to Darkus it was a soup of possibilities.

Then he saw the first sign.

A laminated photograph was attached to the pillar of a small fence. It showed a medium-sized dog with shaggy, light brown hair. Darkus identified it as a Labrador-poodle mix: a Labradoodle as they had become known. This one had what breeders called a cappuccino coat. Its curly hair had been shorn to resemble an unusually soft-hearted lion. Hampstead Heath was evidently its Kalahari. Below the picture was a faded word written in large letters:

LOST

Below that were the words:

Answers to TRIXY ...
Please return for sizeable reward.

Darkus deduced from the description and the age of the sign that Trixy's chances of survival were extremely slim.

Troubled, he spotted another sign a few metres away on the same fence. This laminated photograph showed a Jack Russell terrier. Judging by its taller than average ears, Darkus deduced it was not pure-bred, but a corgi mix. It was a kind, even comical-looking dog. The caption below it also read:

LOST . . . My much loved Bertie.
Please phone if you have any information.

This was more troubling. Jack Russells were known for their intelligence as well as their good humour. They could also be aggressive when provoked. This was not the kind of dog one would normally expect to go missing.

Darkus felt a dull ache in his heart, remembering the pain he'd felt when he thought he was losing Wilbur. Captain Reed's words returned to him: *People let you down . . . but dogs, they never do.*

Darkus walked on, seeing several more laminated signs dotted along the fences. He counted over a dozen missing pets. Judging from the condition of the signs, they had all vanished within the past four to six weeks.

Certain that this was no coincidence, Darkus's mind began to construct possible scenarios for what his father might be pursuing. He thought about the werewolf book and wondered whether (once again) his father had become preoccupied with the supernatural at the expense of a rational explanation. Darkus focused on the matter at hand. First he had to find his father, and hopefully, along the way, he could make sense of the clues that had clearly eluded Knightley Senior to this point.

Darkus turned away from the missing pet photos and found himself at a junction of three footpaths all leading in different directions. A large concrete bin was located at the intersection. Darkus picked up a stick, peered inside the bin and delved through the assortment of rubbish until he spotted a small orange peel, which was almost completely intact. Without doubt, it had belonged to his father. Darkus surveyed the three options, and guessed that his father would have taken the larger, more trafficked footpath that led between the ponds and up into an area of woodland. A fitting habitat for any predator.

Darkus followed the footpath, past a few fishermen camped by the pond, then climbed a steep incline, flanked by dense woods and tall, elderly trees. The shadows were deep and dappled with only occasional rays of sunlight that merely served to illuminate a tangle of creepers and a carpet of dead leaves. Although he was near the centre of London, there was a sense that almost anything could lurk in this terrain, virtually unnoticed. He could only guess how it felt at night, when the animals reclaimed their kingdom, foraging for whatever was left behind; and only the brave, foolhardy or misguided human would dare venture on to their territory.

A row of elegant, Victorian semi-detached houses loomed through the undergrowth, tucked away safely behind high fences. Their only contact with the unknown would be foxes scaling the perimeter in the dead of night to hunt for scraps. That is, unless it was one of their well-heeled pets who had gone missing.

Darkus reached the top of the wooded footpath, finding another intersection: one path curved to the left, leading further into the woods; another led to the right, revealing the base of the vast, grassy ridge known as Parliament Hill.

He chose the well-trodden path leading to Parliament Hill and soon spotted a concrete bin ahead. After probing the contents with the stick, he was rewarded with another almost intact piece of orange peel: he was on the right track. Feeling emboldened, Darkus plodded up the steep slope, which seemingly led straight into the clouds, for there was nothing else beyond the horizon. Reaching the top of Parliament Hill, the landscape unfolded to reveal the full scale of the park, stretching in all directions; and below it, a vast swathe of the capital, which at this height had been reduced to a miniature play city, complete with the Shard, the

Gherkin and the London Eye. Darkus remembered reading that this was where Guy Fawkes and his co-conspirators had planned to watch the Houses of Parliament explode during the Gunpowder Plot on the fifth of November, 1605. Darkus had to admit it would have been the perfect spot. Fortunately that plot had been thwarted, the Houses of Parliament survived, and Fawkes, unfortunately for him, was sentenced to be hung, drawn and quartered – although, being quick-witted to the last, Fawkes had thrown himself from the scaffold, swiftly breaking his neck, to avoid being alive for the drawing and quartering section of his punishment. A very logical decision.

Darkus turned away from the stunning view and approached another concrete bin – which would hopefully provide confirmation of the route. He poked around inside. There were several confectionery wrappers, some dog refuse bags, but no sign of an orange peel. Disappointed, Darkus reached in his coat for a small pair of binoculars and surveyed the Heath from his new vantage point. He panned past several walkers, one of whom glanced back and obviously thought Darkus was spying on him, for he pulled up the collar of his Barbour jacket self-consciously and limped away. Darkus continued panning, zeroing in on another concrete bin at the base of the hill by the edge of the woods.

He pocketed his binoculars and trudged back down Parliament Hill, hoping his earlier blunder would be absolved. After a few minutes he arrived at the bin and smiled, spotting a telltale orange peel – and knowing that his powers of deduction were also intact.

He followed the path around the base of the hill, through a gap in the undergrowth, revealing a lush meadow with a view of a spire in the distance. A fallen tree lay dramatically across one side of the field. Darkus arrived at the next concrete bin – but it held no reward.

Foxed, Darkus retraced his steps and studied the terrain again, noticing a small opening directly behind him, leading back into the woods. Attached to the branch of a thorny bush guarding this opening was a small strand of fibre waving in the wind. Darkus fished out a pair of tweezers and approached the fibre, which was so fine it was almost translucent. He carefully unwound it from the thorn and held it up to the light, comparing it to his own jacket sleeve. The fibres were the same: this was undoubtedly Donegal tweed.

Darkus pocketed the strand, then used the tweezers to pry open the thorny gateway to the woods, revealing a clearing.

The ground was demarcated by a wall of tall thickets, and lying in the centre of the clearing was another orange peel. However, that was not the only clue left behind.

For beside it was an incredibly large, but unmistakable, *paw* print. Whatever had left it was a canine of some kind. A gigantic one. The paw print was heading in the direction of a muddy patch of ground where any other prints that might have been there had long perished. A quick survey confirmed there were no matching markings anywhere in the clearing.

Darkus got out his phone, along with a small plastic ruler. He laid the ruler on the ground beside the paw print and photographed it from several angles to show scale.

Then he spun round, hearing a rustle from somewhere in the undergrowth. His catastophiser started gyrating and rattling, threatening to fall out of its imaginary cradle. He felt his bladder weaken a little and tasted that familiar metallic feeling in his mouth as the adrenalin was released to fuel that most primitive of responses: fight or flight. Then a small bird hopped out of a tree and flew off through the narrow gateway back into the daylight. And the rustling noise was gone.

Darkus steadied his breathing and decided to follow the bird's lead, heading away from the clearing, which had suddenly taken on a sense of foreboding, even terror. But before he left, he spotted a small, silver reflection coming from behind a hedgerow. He approached it slowly, then knelt down and used his tweezers to pick up a dog tag with a small shred of leather collar still attached to it. It had a phone number and a single word engraved on it: *Bertie.*

Darkus returned the way he'd come, dialled the number and regretfully informed the elderly male owner that Bertie had seemingly fallen foul of an indigenous mammal or bird, and was, almost certainly, deceased. Darkus offered to leave the dog tag by the fence below the missing sign, for the owner to retrieve that afternoon. Darkus felt this was essential for achieving a sense of closure. Overcome with emotion, the owner thanked him and hung up.

Having found no more orange peels and no further clues to his father's current location, Darkus walked into Hampstead Village to find a sandwich, preferably a triangular one. He explored the high street, which was lined with coffee shops, boutiques and mobile phone stores, all of which felt a million miles from the wilds of the Heath, even though it was only a few minutes away. He passed a line of tourists queuing up at a French crêpe seller, then continued uphill, past the Tube station, until he stopped and silently cursed his foolishness. Just ahead of him, nestled among the row of shops, was a Pizza Express.

Darkus approached the entrance and saw his father, Alan Knightley, waving to him from a window table. Darkus straightened up in surprise, then bowed his head and entered the restaurant.

'You took your time, Doc,' Knightley declared, beckoning him to the table. 'I hope you don't mind, I started without you.'

Darkus saw what looked like the remains of an 'American Hot' on his father's plate. His father was wearing his trademark tweed ensemble, but instead of a herringbone coat, a waxed Barbour jacket was slung over the back of his chair, and a matching hunter hat perched atop it. Sitting at the opposite place setting was a slightly cold-looking 'Pomodoro Pesto Romana': Darkus's favourite.

'How did you know I was here . . . ?' Darkus marvelled, taking a seat in front of the cold pizza.

'I saw you on Parliament Hill. You really ought to be more careful.'

'The man with the limp.' Darkus recalled the distant figure turning up his collar.

'Yours truly,' Knightley said with a pizza-eating grin.

'You ought to be more careful yourself,' Darkus replied.

'I knew you'd find me. I just thought you'd do it a little faster and more efficiently.'

Darkus grimaced. 'And what if I *hadn't* found you?'

'I suppose I'd have had an extra pizza.'

Darkus looked down at his plate, troubled. After the roller coaster of events that had formed their first adventure he had stupidly believed that his father now considered him an equal partner, someone to be trusted and relied upon. But in fact the world had inexplicably turned back in time to the bad old days when his father saw him as little more than a curiosity. Following Knightley Senior's four-year coma and his attendant memory lapses, Darkus had served as a reference manual for his dad's earlier exploits, which were now stored like trophies in his thirteen-year-old head, in the form of 'the Knowledge'. The Knowledge was the collection of case histories mapping his father's twenty-year career as London's top private detective – even if recently Knightley had come to rely more on his son than he cared to admit. The Knowledge was what had got Darkus into this predicament in the first place, giving him a near-encyclopaedic understanding of crime, criminals and how to apprehend them using the powers of deduction. And Darkus firmly believed that his exclusion from the family business was the very reason Knightley was floundering with whatever this present case turned out to be.

Knightley nodded towards the pizza, a little guiltily. 'You'd better hurry up. It's not getting any warmer.'

Darkus picked up a knife and fork, cut a slice and folded it into his mouth. Although it was cold, the pizza tasted good, as it always did.

'So what *were* you doing on Hampstead Heath?' Darkus asked in between mouthfuls.

'What d'you think I was doing? Hunting a werewolf of course.'

Darkus nodded, resigned to his father's outlandish obsessions. 'Then why didn't you tell me?'

'Because you don't believe in werewolves.'

'Maybe I do.'

'Come, come, Doc. Don't be childish,' he said with no hint of irony. 'We both know what you believe – and I quote: "There's always a rational explanation rather than a supernatural one". Apart from in *this* case obviously. I refer to the paw print you no doubt saw in that wooded clearing.'

'I recorded the evidence, yes.'

'I know of no animal on record with a print that resembles *that*. Do you?' enquired Knightley.

'Not immediately, no.'

'*Quod erat demonstrandum*,' his father said, resting his case.

'Not necessarily,' Darkus countered.

'Must we indulge in this idle back-and-forth in the absence of any evidence to the contrary?'

'Clearly your investigation has drawn a blank. Those missing posters have been there for over a month.'

Knightley frowned. 'I'm aware of that, Doc.'

'More importantly, I hear Uncle Bill is out of play, in hospital recovering from serious injuries.'

'Sadly, that is correct,' admitted Knightley. 'But it's not yet clear if these two cases are related.'

'What happened to him?' Darkus demanded.

'That's not relevant at this point.' Knightley avoided the issue. 'It could be coincidence.'

'I never succumb to the luxury of coincidence,' said Darkus, feeling increasingly frustrated. 'You taught me that.'

'You're going to have to bow to my age and wisdom on this, Doc. I must focus my energies on the matter at hand.'

'Well, maybe I can be of service. You might have forgotten . . .' He slid a business card across the table. 'It says . . . *and Son*.'

'If you'd like to interview one of my witnesses before you shoot down my werewolf theory, be my guest.'

'When and where can I interview this he, she . . . or it?'

Knightley checked his wristwatch. 'We can meet him in exactly twenty minutes, if you'd like?'

Darkus had no idea how his father could be so precise, but he shrugged his consent. 'There's no time like the present.'

Knightley turned to the waitress and called out: 'Two portions of chocolate fudge cake and the bill, please.'

Chapter 5
A SHAGGY DOG STORY

The climb back up Parliament Hill was infinitely more challenging after having consumed a pizza and a thick slice of chocolate fudge cake. Darkus and his dad were both nursing a stitch by the time they reached the summit.

'And how is your mother?' Knightley enquired, with his usual attempt at indifference. But Darkus knew his father's tone well enough to hear the keen interest disguised under the surface.

'She's OK,' he replied, not knowing quite where this line of questioning was going. 'She's been spending time with Wilbur – well, she was, until he was evicted.'

'Clive . . .' Knightley nodded evenly.

'He and Wilbur just never . . . clicked.'

'Well, there's a surprise.'

'Sometimes I don't know why Mum . . .' Darkus trailed off.

'I'm sure she has her reasons, Doc,' his father explained. 'She's loyal to a fault. It takes a lot to drive your mother away. But I managed it, didn't I.'

'The "episode", your condition, it wasn't your fault,' Darkus went on.

'A great many things *were* my fault though. Still, I hope I'll have a chance to make it up to you. To both of you.'

'Good day, Mr Knightley,' a female voice interrupted them.

Darkus turned to see an imposing figure approaching from a side path, surrounded by dogs of all shapes and sizes. It was a large, dramatically shaped woman in her fifties, hemmed in by a tweed jacket and a long plaid skirt. Her white hair was tied back under a silk Hermès headscarf, framing a striking face and a pair of rose-tinted granny spectacles. A sports whistle hung on her chest. The tight ring of golden retrievers, collies and terriers that encircled her sturdy Hunter boots almost gave the impression she was floating on a cloud.

'Is that your witness?' Darkus asked uncertainly.

'No,' Knightley replied. 'An acquaintance from the Heath.'

Darkus did a double take, realising who it was.

'That's Fiona Connelly, from *Bad Dog*,' he murmured, a little star-struck. She looked even more commanding than she did on TV.

'The very same,' answered Knightley with a hint of pride. 'Fiona, meet my son, Darkus. You can call him Doc.'

'Hello, Doc,' she cooed in her dainty but strict upper-class accent, then turned to address his father. 'Mr Knightley, I wonder if I might trouble you for a sit-down sometime soon.' She felt a tug and turned aside to one poorly behaved Labrador. 'Sssssssit!' She blew her whistle so loudly that it gave everyone a start. Then she returned her attention to Knightley, lowering her voice. 'I have a little . . . *problem*, Alan, which I wonder if you might be able to assist with.'

'Fire away. You're in good company. My son sometimes works with me . . .' He searched for an apt description. 'Sort of like an intern.'

Darkus shot his father a look.

Fiona continued: 'It's a little . . . inappropriate to discuss it in front of a child.'

'Technically, I'm a teenager,' Darkus chimed in. 'And by the way, I'm a big fan of your work.'

'How very kind of you. But I would still prefer a *private* session,' she trilled, 'if you wouldn't object, Alan.' She raised an eyebrow, revealing a gummy smile. 'Don't make me beg.'

'Very well,' said Knightley and handed her a card. 'Call my office and I'll be happy to arrange a time.'

'Thank you, I'll do that. *Come*, my darlings!!'

She pointed to the other side of the hill, blew her whistle and the parade of four-legged friends followed behind her with unquestioning loyalty.

'Wow,' uttered Darkus. 'Do you think she does private classes?'

'If we play our cards right, who knows.'

'So where's your witness . . . ?'

Knightley pointed to a middle-aged man with a shock of long, grey hair and a pair of heavily bristling sideburns. He was dressed in slightly over-tight spandex, with a bandana tied around his head, and was performing a series of Tai Chi exercises on a small mound. He swept his arms around, then brought them close to his chest, occasionally raising a knee or extending into a stretch. Darkus noted the similarities to the Knightleys' own chosen martial art, Wing Chun, which also relied on the movement of energy – but in the Knightleys' case it involved deflecting an enemy's energy and returning it in the form of a punch.

An ageing but loyal collie appeared from the blind side of the hill, also wearing a bandana, and dropped a frisbee at the Tai Chi man's feet. The close resemblance between dog and owner was a phenomenon Darkus had seen on many occasions, but in this case the likeness was uncanny. Without breaking his rhythm, the man reached down for the frisbee and elegantly hurled it down the hill for the dog to fetch. The dog fled after it, leaving the man to continue his exercises.

'Him?' whispered Darkus.

His father nodded.

'I hope you brought your silver bullets,' Darkus quipped.

'I'm still working on those, although there's no first-hand evidence that they actually do kill werewolves,' Knightley responded, perfectly serious. 'Excuse me, sir?' he called out.

'Is there something more I can help you with?' the Tai Chi man replied, his voice fading in the wind.

'My son would like to hear your testimony,' Knightley went on.

'He's only a kid, man,' the Tai Chi man replied, examining Darkus with scepticism.

'Yes, but with a thirst for knowledge,' replied Knightley. 'Be good enough to tell him what you saw at the last full moon.'

Darkus examined the witness carefully for any facial tics or tells.

The Tai Chi man reached in his spandex jacket for a tobacco pouch. 'I come up here the same time every day. Good for the mind, body and soul,' he advised, rolling up a cigarette, raising it to his mouth and lighting it.

Darkus had observed these sorts of contradictions before: sports masters who ate too much; doctors who drank too much; Uncle Bill who did all of the above too much. But he didn't think this would disparage the witness's testimony – if what the man had to say was even sensible.

'Proceed,' said Darkus.

'Well, I was up here last month, and I decided to stay late, and the moon was high and full. I was practising my form, inhaling through my nostrils, drawing colourless energy from the earth, through my ancient roots, up my sushumna channel and into my sacral chakra. You dig?'

'I dig,' Knightley replied.

'Then I blew out the dark, toxic energy through my mouth. Great clouds of it.'

'Go on,' prompted Darkus, raising his eyebrows and glancing at his father.

Knightley shrugged.

The Tai Chi man went on. 'Well, Puja noticed it first.'

'Puja?' Darkus asked.

'The dog,' he replied, pointing down to the collie, who had still not located the frisbee, even though it was bright red and lying in plain sight.

'What did she notice exactly?' Darkus went on.

'She started barking at the trees,' he replied.

'Which trees precisely?' said Darkus.

'All of them. She kept turning round in circles, barking in all directions.'

Darkus surveyed the Heath from this high position: there were acres of trees extending on all sides.

'What d'you think she was barking at?' he asked.

'Something was moving in them,' the man answered. 'I couldn't see what. But it's like the trees themselves were *moving*.'

'The wind perhaps?' Darkus suggested.

'It was going too fast for that. It was *in* the trees. Let's just say, it wasn't *of nature*.'

'Did you get a look at this entity?' asked Darkus. 'Can you give us a description?'

'Nope. We ran when we heard the howl.'

'The howl?'

'Most mind-blowingly terrifying noise I ever heard in my life,' the witness stammered. 'Puja bolted and I was right behind her. Didn't stop running till we reached the pub.'

Darkus nodded. 'I see. And have you ever witnessed this phenomenon since that time?'

'Guess we'll have to wait until the next full moon. But when it comes, you sure as hell won't find me up here.' He spread his feet shoulder-width apart, closed his eyes and returned to his exercises.

Knightley accompanied his son away from the mound.

'Well?' Knightley asked impatiently. 'What d'you think?'

'It's too early to say,' Darkus responded.

'Don't give me that line. I invented that line.'

'Well, he's hardly the most reliable witness.'

'I thought you would've learned from our last investigation,' said Knightley, 'that you can't judge a book by its cover.'

'My mind is open to every possibility. Even the most outlandish one.'

'You're not a very good liar, Doc,' his father commented. 'You'll find that comes with age and experience.'

Darkus furrowed his brow, not wishing to face the spectre of adulthood just yet. His father had made plenty of mistakes: losing Darkus's mum Jackie to the interloper, Clive; and losing many of his detective skills during the four-year coma, which had ultimately led to Darkus and his father teaming up as partners in solving crime. Darkus would make plenty of mistakes too – but hopefully on his own schedule, not his father's.

Knightley appealed to him again. 'If you don't believe this man's testimony, and I can't say I blame you,' he admitted, 'may I suggest we visit someone whose judgement you *do* trust? Or at least . . . sort of?'

Chapter 6
A RELATIVE ONCE REMOVED

'Did ye bring the bickies, Alan?' Uncle Bill blurted, attempting to sit up in his hospital bed. He eventually resorted to pressing a button, which raised him like an overweight Count Dracula back from the dead. Without his hat and overcoat, Bill was deprived of some of his enigma, but none of his girth, which seemed to have experienced a growth spurt, or girth spurt – presumably due to a period of inactivity, regular hospital meals and sympathy gifts of confectionery – and as a result, his patient's gown was struggling to conceal him.

Two nurses hurried to his aid, one adjusting his gown while another poured him a cup of water. An armed policeman stood in silence, guarding the door.

'Don't over-exert yourself, Mr Billoch,' one of the nurses cautioned, using Bill's real name.

'Aye, Bill, listen tae the hen,' said an equally huge

man from a cramped seat in the corner. 'And for God's sake cut doon on the swedgers.'

'Ah, dinnae fash yerself!' Bill retorted.

'Dougal,' said Knightley, addressing the extra Scotsman in the room. 'I don't believe you and Doc have been formally introduced.'

Darkus did a double take: the likeness between Dougal and Bill was quite extraordinary. Apparently Dougal was the younger brother, although they looked exactly the same age.

Dougal raised himself to his feet, doffed his homburg hat and shook Darkus's hand in his giant paw. 'I've heard a lot about ye, Doc.'

'All good, I hope,' replied Darkus.

'Vairy impressive wark on the last case,' Dougal responded, although it took Darkus a moment to translate.

Knightley approached the bed. 'What's the prognosis, Bill?'

'The docs tell me mah calf is nearly healed up,' said Bill. 'They had tae dae a skin graft from mah . . . Well, I cannae go into tha' nou, Alan. Nae in front ay young Darkus.'

'Agreed,' said Knightley.

'Nou, Doc,' Bill went on. 'How are ye? How's skale?'

'Let's just say I prefer the university of life. Or of criminal investigation, in my case,' Darkus replied.

Bill turned to Knightley proudly. 'Aye, he hasn't changed a bit, has he?' Knightley shook his head. 'Well, what can ah dae for ye tway gents?' Bill asked.

'Doc's here to talk to you about the incident at the Thames,' Knightley began.

'Aye, you mean the beastie,' replied Bill. 'It was dark, but ah believe it was a werewolf, Doc, as far as ah could tell. It was tae clever tae be a normal doggy. Tae cunning.'

Dougal snorted from the corner, but it was unclear whether it was in response to Bill or not.

Darkus couldn't help thinking about the two dogs that had staked out Clive and Jackie's house on Wolseley Close the previous night. What were these sentient canines? Where were they coming from? And what did they want?

'Ye see, it was as if the beastie was *only* interested in *me*,' Bill continued. 'It didn't change course once, and was nae interested in my chocolate Penguin biscuit neither. A terrible waste that was,' he mourned.

Darkus and his dad exchanged glances.

Knightley added, 'Bill's under police protection here until we can get to the bottom of who, or what, was targeting them.'

'Them?' enquired Darkus.

'That same night, during the full moon, three other senior Scotland Yard officers were viciously mauled, and later succumbed to their injuries.'

'Aye,' Bill interjected. 'Had their throats torn oot, poor fowk.'

Darkus understood. 'Wait, you mean the three officers in south London responding to a domestic altercation? I saw it on the news a few weeks ago. It said they were attacked by a tenant's dog.'

'That was a cover story,' Knightley explained. 'The officers were actually in three separate London locations, each returning home from the same high-level meeting of SO 42.'

'Bill's department. Specialist Operations 42. The Department of the Unexplained,' Darkus murmured.

'Correct,' said Knightley.

'What was this high-level meeting about?'

'An unexplained rise in gang crime and aggressive dogs across the capital.' Knightley gestured through the window to the sun sinking over the London skyline.

Darkus took a moment to process all this, then whispered to his father privately: 'And you believe there's a connection between this and the missing pets on Hampstead Heath . . . ?'

Knightley nodded uncertainly. 'I do, Doc, I just haven't worked out what that connection is yet.'

'And I suppose you believe the Combination is involved.'

'You read my mind. Nothing on this scale could escape their controlling grasp.'

'But Morton Underwood, their leader, is dead.'

'Their leadership is a revolving door, Doc. I told you that. Besides, I'm not convinced your former godfather is dead.'

'He fell under a train. I saw it with my own eyes.'

'But Morton's body was never recovered.'

Darkus took a breath, trying to stay in the here and now. 'This is all getting too far ahead of the evidence. We have no motive, no perpetrator, no dog.'

'Nae werewolf,' added Bill.

Dougal snorted again, and Darkus realised the Scotsman had in fact fallen asleep.

'What I dae have is an artist's impression of the beast,' Bill said, extracting a crumpled piece of paper from his bedclothes and holding it up.

It was little more than a cartoon scribbled down with a Sharpie. Darkus examined the sketch, deeming it too crude to be of any use. It could have depicted the dogs he'd seen on Wolseley Close – or it could have depicted a particularly angry glove puppet.

A nurse interrupted them. 'Mr Billoch needs his rest.'

Bill shrugged as another nurse plumped up his cushions. 'What can ah do?'

Knightley fished in his jacket, took out a packet of chocolate digestives and set them on the bedside table.

'Classic or new recipe?' Bill asked quietly.

'Classic, of course,' answered Knightley.

'Yoo're mah Florence Nightingale, Alan,' purred Bill.

'Ah told ye, nae bannocks,' Dougal piped up.

'Haud yer wheesht!' snapped Bill.

'I suggest we get back to the office,' Knightley told his son. 'There might be time for a round of jam sandwiches, triangles not squares, naturally, then it's an early night, wake up for a full English, say your goodbyes to Wilbur – for now of course – and take the first train home.'

Something about his father's announcement didn't ring true. It was as if they both knew, one or way or another, the train would not be caught and Darkus would not be going home – at least not yet.

'Dad, you know full well I can't leave in the middle of a case,' Darkus remonstrated. 'That is unless you want it to remain in the vaults of the Department of the Unexplained, rather than have it put before a jury and see justice done.'

'You do make a strong case, Doc.'

'I know. I learned from the best.'

'Flattery will get you everywhere. But there is one overriding issue that you have patently ignored, and I fear you will have no adequate answer for. And that is your *mother*. I imagine she's expecting a call within the hour, and you home by tomorrow night.'

'Can you tell her I'm unwell?' Darkus suggested.

'She won't buy it.'

'I thought you said you were a good liar.'

'Not that good.'

'Then perhaps we should offer her the truth,' said Darkus.

'And that is?'

'That you're out of your depth. Again.' His father frowned, his brow creasing. Darkus continued regardless: 'And that without my assistance you may fall victim to another "episode", or worse.'

'The delivery was unnecessarily cruel, Doc. But, as usual, I fear you may be on to something.'

'She does care about you, Dad. Whether she admits it or not.'

Knightley pursed his lips and made an odd chomping expression as he digested this last piece of evidence, before coming to a decision. 'Let's hope you're right.'

Chapter 7
THE DOG WHISPERER

If Darkus had any doubts about Wilbur's new digs, they were quickly dispelled when he and his father returned to 27 Cherwell Place that evening to find Bogna and the mutt had already become bosom buddies.

After greeting the Knightleys with an unusual level of affection – wagging his tail several times as opposed to the usual single wag – Wilbur returned to Bogna's lap, literally leaping on to her as she sat in an armchair following a particularly gruelling session with the Hoover. Bogna didn't seem to mind this furry lump using her as an improvised dog basket. In fact she appeared to like it.

'Good boyee, Wilburs. Now show Alan and Darkus what Bogna teach you.'

Wilbur raised his eyebrows as if to say: Do I have to?

'Don't make argument with me, Wilburs.'

Wilbur frowned, twitched his whiskers, then lowered one, two, then all four legs to the carpet. He then walked to the centre of the living room and sat perfectly still, back straight, head held high.

Darkus watched in amazement, then looked to his father for confirmation. Knightley narrowed his eyes to examine the phenomenon.

Bogna resumed her tuition. 'Good. Now fetch Bogna the feathered duster.' Wilbur cocked his head reluctantly. 'Go . . .' she urged.

Wilbur slowly got back to his feet and trotted into the kitchen, vanishing behind the fridge. A moment later he returned, carrying the feather duster gingerly between his teeth. He raised his snout, handing it to Bogna, who duly nodded and held it vertically in her right hand, briefly resembling a monarch upon the throne holding a sceptre.

'Outstanding,' remarked Knightley.

'It's incredible,' agreed Darkus.

Bogna casually shrugged. 'Now, Wilburs . . . Bogna is feelings hungry. Fetch Bogna something for eats.'

Wilbur wagged his tail, trotted back to the fridge, sat on his haunches and extended his back, reaching out with his right paw. He pulled on the handle and the fridge door swung open. Wilbur then staggered forward on his hind legs, gently resting his paws against the shelf of the fridge and carefully taking a small box of chocolates between his teeth. He staggered backwards, sat on his haunches again, closed the door with his paw and returned to Bogna, wagging his tail.

Bogna took the chocolate box from his jaws. 'Good boyee. Now, feets?' She nodded to the ottoman, which Wilbur obediently nudged into position as she lowered her Crocs on to it, for ultimate relaxation.

As she selected a chocolate from the box and popped it in her mouth, Darkus and his dad exchanged an even deeper look of disbelief.

'How did you do it?' asked Darkus, struggling to comprehend how it took Bogna one day to achieve what he had failed to do in three months.

'You don't like?' she replied, concerned.

'No. It's amazing,' said Darkus. 'You could put Fiona Connelly out of business.'

Bogna bit down on a particularly chewy chocolate piece. 'I just talk to him like normals adult.' She cocked her head and swallowed. 'I say gets me this, he gets me that.'

'It's his training,' Knightley added under his breath. 'It must be coming back. Wilbur is clearly a very clever dog under his rather dysfunctional exterior. I'm confident he may yet be of some use to us.'

Darkus checked his simple Timex watch and frowned. Knightley caught his look and nodded.

'To business,' said Knightley and led his son upstairs.

They entered the office, closing the door behind them. Knightley took up position behind his mahogany desk while Darkus pulled up a chair, took out his secure phone and dialled. After a few rings Jackie picked up.

'Doc?' she asked anxiously. 'Is everything OK?'

'I'm fine, Mum. But I'm afraid I won't be coming home tomorrow.'

'But – what about school?'

'I suggest you tell them I'm ill,' he advised. 'Sorry, but I have to ask you to be economical with the truth.'

'You mean lie,' she replied bluntly.

'For good reasons, yes,' said Darkus, then paused, summoning the courage to confess. 'Dad needs my help again.'

He was met with stony silence on the other end of the line. Then Jackie's voice wavered, not wanting to believe that history was repeating itself.

'Put your father on the phone, Doc,' she said sternly.

'OK, Mum.' Darkus passed the phone to his dad.

'Hello, Jackie,' Knightley began cheerily, until he was cut off by her response, which Darkus could imagine, but couldn't hear. 'Well, actually, it was *his* idea –' Knightley replied, until he was cut off again.

Not wishing to listen to this awkward altercation, and finding it strangely familiar from the days when they were a complete, if eccentric, family, Darkus walked to the landing window and glanced down at Cherwell Place. The Victorian street lamps flickered to life, one by one. A light mist crept around the lanterns as it was wont to do.

Darkus tuned out the sound of his parents arguing, then felt something brush against him. He started, and looked down to see Wilbur nuzzling his trouser leg restlessly, before raising his snout, as if sniffing for trouble.

'What is it, boy?'

Wilbur made some apprehensive puffing noises, then reared back and raised his front paws to rest on the window ledge, beside Darkus.

Darkus followed his line of sight and spotted two low, muscular shapes appearing from the mist at the end of the road, dimly lit by the street lamps which were still warming up. Darkus instantly recognised the shapes as canines – their torsos jet black and teeming with sinews and tendons: most likely a Rottweiler-wolf mix. Not so different to Bill's crude sketch – if one used some imagination. As the dogs trotted along the pavement in a perfectly matching half-step, Darkus drew closer to the windowpane. Uncannily, the pair looked identical to the dogs that had been conducting surveillance at Wolseley Close just the night before.

Darkus and Wilbur watched as the two dogs came to a halt in the circle of light under the street lamp located outside number 27. The dogs turned to look at each other, as if they were in some sort of silent conversation, like co-conspirators – they appeared almost human in the subtlety of their expression. Both dogs directed their gaze upwards to the office. Darkus immediately flicked the light switch off, so he and Wilbur could observe unseen.

'What are they *doing* here . . . ?' Darkus uttered under his breath. 'What are they sniffing around for?'

Wilbur let out a low growl and his tail sank fearfully between his legs.

The dogs gazed up at the office for another full thirty seconds, then appeared to nod at each other and trotted away with identical purpose, but in opposite directions. Darkus squinted to check his eyes hadn't deceived him.

Within moments, the dogs had exited from opposing ends of the street.

Darkus took a moment to process this nonsensical evidence, then confidently re-entered the office, closely followed by Wilbur.

His father was in mid-speech: 'I promised once, and I'll promise you again, Jackie. I won't let any harm come to him . . .'

'Dad, I need to speak to Mum,' Darkus interjected with certainty.

'Hold on a tick –' said Knightley, attempting to bring her to a halt. 'Doc wants to speak to you.' He shrugged and passed the phone guiltily back to Darkus.

'Mum, I'm sorry to do this . . . again,' he admitted, knowing how unfair it was on her. 'But in the light of recent events I am now convinced the game is – once again – afoot, and Dad needs my help . . . more than ever.'

Her voice came through the handset. 'Darkus, I know how loyal you are to your dad, and I respect that. But you're still a child –'

'Mum, listen to me. For the moment, my being at Wolseley Close is not safe, not for *me* . . . not for *you*, Clive or Tilly. Something is going on, and until I work out what it is, I'm staying in London with Dad.'

'And I suppose I have no say in this?' she argued.

'You trusted me once. Just trust me again.'

'What d'you expect me to say, Darkus?' Jackie's voice wavered with emotion. 'If I agree I'm putting you in harm's way, and if I refuse –'

'You'll be doing the exact same thing,' Darkus answered for her.

'So what am I meant to do?' she asked helplessly.

'Call Cranston on Monday. Be as convincing as you can. Tell them I'm suffering a bout of seasonal influenza, my temperature is fluctuating between thirty-nine and forty-one degrees, my glands are up and you've confined me to bed rest for the next few days. At least until the full moon.'

Knightley raised his eyebrows, realising his son was now, without question, on the case.

'Until the full moon . . . ?' Jackie asked, incredulous.

Darkus realised he'd said too much. 'Yes. I believe I will have completed my work here by then. Thanks for understanding, Mum.'

'Wait, Darkus –'

'The trail is getting cold, Mum. I love you. I'll keep my phone on whenever I can, as long as it doesn't compromise the investigation. Bye for now.' Darkus winced and ended the call, then looked up at his dad.

'She'll understand,' said Knightley in an attempt at reassurance. 'It's me she won't forgive.'

'I'm more concerned by our current predicament,' said Darkus. 'Have you noticed a pair of dogs conducting surveillance on the office?'

'Dogs? Conducting surveillance?'

'I believe so, yes,' said Darkus.

'I've seen nothing of the kind.'

'Then I must assume they've either eluded your attention, or they have somehow followed me from Wolseley Close – incredible as that may sound.'

'You saw them there as well?' asked Knightley, astonished.

Darkus nodded. 'Last night . . . And they're no ordinary canines. They appear to be a particularly aggressive-looking Rottweiler mix.' Darkus hesitated, before proceeding with testimony that he knew full well would provide a lit match to his father's most explosive and far-fetched ideas. 'I only have visual evidence, in poor light, but I believe – irrational as it sounds – that these dogs are able to communicate with each other, possibly in an operational capacity.'

'You mean they're "smart" dogs?' Knightley's ears pricked up.

'It would appear so. The question is . . . what do they want with us?'

'The question is . . .' Knightley weighed in, 'are we in fact dealing with more than one werewolf . . . ?' He pondered a moment. 'Think about the attacks on the police. The missing pets on the Heath.'

Darkus shook his head. 'I would prefer to stay in the realm of reality, not the supernatural. We don't even know that the cases are linked.'

'The evidence will determine which one of us is residing in reality, Doc,' said Knightley, then sat back in his chair and massaged his brow, as if waiting for an answer to present itself. 'Well, what are your theories?' he submitted.

'Based on the evidence, Dad,' Darkus began, 'the paw print we found at Hampstead Heath cannot be a match for the prints of the dogs that have been watching us. The print from the Heath was far larger in size and far more unusual in toe spread and angle of footfall. Therefore, I can conclude that these two lines of investigation are – so far – *un*related.'

'It's too early to make that assumption,' Knightley reprimanded him. 'The soil may have been corrupted. The Heath is three hundred and twenty hectares large. There must be more prints out there.' Knightley's eyes lit up wildly. 'Given time and resources, we may be able to find them.'

Darkus realised he was yet again engaged in the same old dispute with his father: namely, would the five senses account for every unexplained incident in the world; or, in some cases, does the occult provide the only solution, however improbable it might seem?

'As you say,' Darkus continued, 'the Heath is the size of a small town. It would be like looking for a needle . . . in a small town. Besides, I see no reason to force the square peg of a mythical werewolf into the round hole of this investigation. So far, there is no empirical connection. Our immediate problem is that we appear to be under surveillance by a pair of very clever canines.'

'So what d'you recommend we do about it?'

'Simple. We use counter-surveillance,' Darkus replied.

'You mean cameras?' Knightley remarked. Darkus shook his head in response. 'Then what . . . ?'

Wilbur trotted into the middle of the room and sat perfectly upright.

'You're looking at him,' said Darkus, nodding to the dog. 'Wilbur can tell us when they're here,' Darkus announced. 'He can *smell* them.'

'Your reasoning is sound,' admitted Knightley.

Darkus steepled his fingers and narrowed his gaze. 'Once he has the scent, we might even be able to *track* them.'

Chapter 8
AN EARLY MORNING WALK

Later that evening, the Knightleys found their senses overpowered by the characteristically pungent aroma of Bogna's traditional Polish cooking. After a meal of *bigos* (hunter's stew) consisting of boiled cabbage, boiled sausage and boiled onions, which could have fed an army, and required several hours to digest (Darkus feared some ingredients would never be fully digested), Knightley ordered his son to set aside the case for the day.

Darkus suspected his father was still holding something back from him, but he couldn't work out what it was; and Darkus knew that if he confronted his dad, he would only clam up further.

The Knightleys retired to their respective bedrooms – Darkus's being the chaise longue in the office. Wilbur opted for the armchair opposite.

*

Darkus and his dog both slept fitfully, with each of them flinching and emitting mumbled communications that were more the result of the unconscious than the conscious. At around five in the morning, Wilbur slipped off the armchair and leaped to his feet, causing Darkus to do the same. Darkus tuned his hearing to cover all possible frequencies, finding one wavelength that contained the rumbling, bronchial snores of Bogna; and another that appeared to contain muffled footsteps descending the stairs and quietly closing the front door behind them. Having superior powers of hearing, Wilbur had already darted to the office window; and when Darkus joined him they saw Knightley striding down Cherwell Place towards the alley with the row of garages – one of which contained the black London cab.

Before Darkus could assemble his thoughts, he heard his father's cab stutter, then fire up on all cylinders, exploding into life. Seconds later it accelerated out of the alley and vanished down a side street. Darkus pressed the speed dial on his phone, but, as he suspected, his dad's mobile was switched off. He opened an application on his phone and hailed a black cab online. Then he threw on his clothes and descended the stairs. As he took the collar and lead from a coat hook, Wilbur cried with excitement, until Darkus hushed him, for fear of alerting Bogna. Fortunately her rumbling snores were undisturbed.

Darkus closed the front door behind him and led Wilbur towards the waiting cab. He was tempted to say 'Follow that car', but realised his father was already long gone.

The cabbie leaned out of the window and pointed to Wilbur. 'He soils the vehicle – you're paying.'

'I give you my personal guarantee, he'll do nothing of the sort,' replied Darkus. 'Now please take us to Hampstead Heath as quickly as possible.' He led Wilbur into the cabin and was thrown back in his seat as the driver hit the accelerator.

During the ride, Darkus thought he saw his father's cab some way ahead, racing through shadowy intersections in the predawn light. But it was too far away to tell if it was Knightley or just another black cab in a hurry, like the one Darkus was now travelling in. Wilbur raised his nose to the half-open window, drinking in the motley array of smells that circulated around the capital in the early hours.

The cabbie drove them up a steep hill, past the Hampstead Heath overground station, arriving at a car park overlooking the fields and ponds. Even at this elevation, the sun was still below the treeline and the capital was veiled in an ominous blue shadow. The cabbie's headlights picked out the empty gravelled lot until, sure enough, Darkus spotted his father's Fairway cab parked diagonally in the corner nearest the park entrance. Whatever the purpose of his early morning visit, his dad clearly wasn't wasting any time.

The rest of the Heath, for as far as the eye could see, was deserted.

Darkus paid the driver, nearly cleaning out his wallet in the process, and led Wilbur out of the rear passenger door. At once, Wilbur raised his snout to the air like a chef distinguishing between minutely different ingredients, then bobbed his nose around as if searching for one scent in particular.

'Dad . . .' prompted Darkus. 'Can you smell him?'

Wilbur cried, trying to reply.

Darkus licked his finger and raised it to the dark sky, feeling the saliva evaporate. 'We're downwind. We're in luck,' he reminded himself. 'Wind carries sound, and smell . . .'

Wilbur barked a response, then led Darkus towards his father's black cab.

Darkus waited patiently, as Wilbur sniffed around the driver side of the car, then the dog's tail stood upright and he started tugging on the lead, urgently pulling Darkus towards a large meadow that spanned the length of the ponds.

Darkus found himself being dragged, running behind Wilbur as they made a beeline across the grassy expanse towards a long, dusty track. Barely able to keep up, Darkus reached down for Wilbur's collar.

'Wilbur, listen to me. If I let you off the lead, don't lose me, OK, boy? OK . . . ?'

Wilbur replied with a two-tone whimper that almost sounded like 'OK.'

Darkus unclipped the lead from the collar, and Wilbur bounded through the long grass, which almost submerged him, except for his tail, which remained bolt upright. He was on the hunt. The dog leaped over the larger patches of undergrowth with what looked like unadulterated joy. Darkus suddenly imagined him as a puppy, surging forward without limitation, without anxiety or fear – as if the world, however big, couldn't contain him. The scared, nervous Wilbur was, for now, a figment of the past. Darkus sprinted to keep up with him, watching the erect tail cut effortlessly through the wilderness like the periscope of a fast attack submarine.

Wilbur appeared on a bluff in the distance, triumphantly raised his snout to the air again, then veered off to the right, joining the dust track that was now clearly in view, leading into a particularly dark cluster of woods.

Incredibly, as Darkus crested the bluff, he saw his father two hundred metres ahead on the same track, his distinctive tweed hat and overcoat blowing in the breeze. As if sensing their presence, Knightley turned around and waved, before shouting out:

'Call him off, Doc. And you too!' His voice carried on the wind.

'Why?!' Darkus shouted back. 'What are you doing here?'

'Looking for more prints of course. This is my case, Doc, leave it to me! I promised your mother I wouldn't let any harm come to you.'

Wilbur was by this time zeroing in on Knightley.

'Dad – wait – !'

'*There was something I didn't show you!*' he shouted hoarsely. 'Call him off, Doc, for both your sakes!' Then Knightley turned and ran off into the woods to elude them.

Wilbur picked up speed to go after him. Darkus froze, then shouted out for fear of losing them both.

'Wilbur! Stop!'

Wilbur came to a halt, then craned his neck to look at his master, not understanding.

'Wait!' Darkus ran along the track, out of breath, catching up with him.

Wilbur's brow furrowed and his nose twitched impatiently – confused at the conflicting commands.

'I know,' Darkus said to the mutt. 'I don't understand him either.'

95

Darkus looked around to discover that they were still very much alone on the Heath. He grabbed a pair of binoculars out of his pocket and trained them down the track and into the woods where his father had just vanished. He adjusted the focus wheel and through the lenses he could just make out his father's tweed coat moving purposefully between the trees, descending into a dell of some kind.

Suddenly, the wind picked up, whistling through the landscape, dislodging loose branches and sending waves of leaves rolling along the ground. Darkus lowered his binoculars, watching the air currents race past him through the meadow.

Wilbur whimpered and his tail sank between his legs. Darkus looked down, confused.

'What is it, boy?'

Inexplicably, Wilbur let out a soft howl that floated up on the breeze. It was plaintive and sad, but it also sounded distinctly like a warning. For that reason it sent shivers up his master's spine and set the catastrophiser whirring.

Darkus pressed his face to the eyecups of the binoculars again, and saw his father's tweed overcoat moving deeper into the forest and further out of sight. Then, to his horror, Darkus saw something else which made the catastophiser jitter so violently that he had trouble steadying his hands, and felt a film of sweat develop between his skin and the binoculars.

Something else was in the woods. Something large that was descending into the dell behind his dad. Darkus fumbled with the focus wheel, but couldn't tell what the thing was, only that it was walking on two legs, and appeared to be a human form.

'Dad!' Darkus spontaneously called out, lowering the binocs for a moment. But his voice was lost on the howling wind.

He pressed his eyes to the lenses again, then panned wildly, but his father, and whatever had been following him, was *gone*.

Darkus clipped the lead to Wilbur's collar and set off down the track and into the woods, looping the leather around his clammy hand for fear of it slipping free. He tried to remember his Wing Chun breathing exercises but they had no effect, and his heart felt like it had travelled up through his body and was beating in the back of his throat.

With unspoken trepidation, Darkus and Wilbur followed the track downhill between several ancient mounds of clay, feeling the temperature drop as they moved into the long shadows of the tree-covered firmament. One after another, they lost their balance on the loose earth, as they descended into the dark heart of the Heath.

They reached the bottom of the dell, where an ancient tree with three gigantic branches, all covered in thick ivy, extended upwards in a devil's fork. Spooked, Darkus held up his binoculars again, scanning the woods, but finding no sign of his dad.

Wilbur pulled him off to one side, past a small footbridge, through a tangle of reeds, following the barren course of a forgotten riverbed. They were moving with stealth, zigzagging to avoid twigs that would break underfoot, until Wilbur led him up a steep incline to an empty clearing surrounded on all sides by a high wall of thickets.

Darkus recognised it as the clearing he'd found the last time he was searching for his dad – only this time they'd approached it from another direction.

Wilbur came to a halt and sat perfectly still. Darkus looked down and noticed Wilbur's nostrils narrowing, and his jowls rising up to bare his teeth in a silent growl. He was facing off with something, but Darkus couldn't work out what it was. Then Darkus's visual faculty was bypassed by another one, as he smelled what Wilbur had already detected.

It was the smell of *death*, plain and simple. The putrid, damp stench of rotting flesh. Darkus attempted to move forward, but Wilbur wouldn't budge.

Darkus followed Wilbur's line of sight and realised on closer inspection that one wall of the clearing was actually a makeshift blockade, constructed out of branches, vines and leaves. How could he not have noticed that before? Darkus tried to lead Wilbur forward, but the dog stayed frozen on the spot like a statue.

Darkus let the lead fall to the ground beside Wilbur, and reluctantly walked forward alone, trying not to let the smell invade his nostrils; but it was impossible, and he felt the foul aroma laying siege to his palate, engulfing his senses and overpowering his brain. He tasted a sour flavour at the back of his throat as his stomach threatened to send its contents back up towards his mouth.

Not wanting to touch anything, he took a silver Parker pen from his top pocket and extended it in front of him like a wand, until it made contact with a curtain of foliage that acted as a doorway – but a doorway into what? The catastrophiser thumped mercilessly, telling him to run away, but curiosity got the better of it.

Darkus gently parted the curtain with the pen and peered in.

The darkness suddenly came alive in a high-pitched chorus of buzzing as hundreds of bluebottle flies flooded through the gap in the curtain, colliding with Darkus's eyes, nose and mouth. He tried to cry out but couldn't for fear of them entering his throat. He pursed his lips, removed his hat and swatted at them as more and more billowed out in black clouds of bristly hair and coarse, veiny wings. He systematically brushed them out of his eyes, nose and ears.

Wilbur turned tail and ran in the opposite direction.

Darkus felt the flies hitting his face, but the torrent seemed to be subsiding a little. He took another step forward, parting the curtain further, until the foliage slid to one side – to reveal what was behind it.

Within seconds, Darkus realised he could no longer control the contents of his stomach and was violently sick on the ground.

Above him, dangling from the makeshift rafters of a cramped, improvised hunting lodge, were dozens of animals – if you could still call them that. They were hung, flayed and disembowelled, all in various states of decomposition – some were only skeletons. Their once pristine fur coats were hung neatly all around, stretched out like perfectly symmetrical butterflies, held in place by sharp, rusted hooks. A few bluebottles still buzzed greedily around the unfortunate victims' carcasses. Darkus had read about the rituals of game hunting, and this was, without doubt, a 'hanging room'. It was unclear whether these poor four-legged souls were trophies or game for the purposes of eating – or perhaps the hunter didn't distinguish between the two.

Darkus thought his stomach had evacuated itself, but he felt another involuntary heave as he rapidly surveyed the contents of the room, mentally accounting for the various foxes, rabbits, terriers and what appeared to be the skins of some much larger dogs: one a golden retriever and one a red setter. Darkus controlled his retches, pulled out his phone and committed the gruesome gallery to his photo album, the flash repeatedly catching the vacant, staring eyes (those fortunate enough to still have them), trapped for ever in the terrifying moment of their untimely demise. Darkus backed out of the foul room, nearly tripping over himself as he went.

He stared at the ground for a moment, steadying his nerves and trying to settle his stomach, until he heard something even more chilling: it was his father's voice, crying out in obvious and uncharacteristic fear.

'Help – ! Somebody – !' Knightley's voice echoed across the woods.

Darkus spun around, feeling the adrenalin surge through his body, setting the catastrophiser to hyper-alert but leaving his limbs as heavy as lead.

'Please – !!' his father shouted.

Darkus instantly traced the source of the noise to the narrow opening in the clearing that led to the path at the base of Parliament Hill.

'Dad!!' he shouted back, as he raced away from the lodge, across the muddy ground and burst through the thorny bushes on to the path. 'Dad? Where are you?!'

Darkus craned his neck left and right, but the path was empty, as was the entire park. Then he heard a scuffling noise and looked up, seeing his father just over a hundred metres away, at the top of Parliament Hill, locked in a life-and-death struggle with a massively built male figure. The figure had Knightley in a stranglehold and was trying to wrestle him to the ground. Despite his opponent's obvious physical advantage, Knightley was still upright, using a series of moves to deflect his opponent's power to the left and right.

Darkus looked around, helpless, then put his fingers to his lips and let out a loud wolf whistle. A second later, Wilbur exploded through a set of bushes behind him and with unspoken purpose they set off up the hill to Knightley's aid.

The image of the fighting silhouettes blurred as Darkus sprinted up the incline, over the uneven ground, feeling the blood running from his head to his feet. His lungs burned and his eyes struggled to focus, creating the illusion that the two figures locked in combat were one amorphous shape. Wilbur was already a good way ahead, leaping over bluffs and homing in on them.

Suddenly, the grappling figures toppled behind the skyline of the hill, out of sight.

'Dad!!' Darkus called out, barely able to breathe.

Wilbur darted over the horizon next, vanishing behind it as well. Then there was a deafening silence. Darkus only heard the noise of his own chest hyperventilating. The catastrophiser was clattering, in bits. He stumbled the last few metres to the summit of the hill and looked over the edge.

The massive figure was gone. Strangely, there was no obvious cover in sight, but still, the figure had completely disappeared. The hill extended down on all sides, with London waking up far in the distance. Darkus saw his father laid out on the grass, motionless.

He ran to where Wilbur was earnestly licking Knightley's face, which was frozen in a look of terror, his eyes wide.

'Dad . . . ?' Darkus shook him, trying to get some reaction – any reaction.

Wilbur withdrew and sat still, looking around, guarding them. Darkus took his father's head in his arms, finding himself cast once again in an all too familiar role.

His father's face slowly relaxed into a look of tacit acceptance and his eyes gently closed, despite his chest heaving and sinking at regular intervals. History was repeating itself. Knightley was, without doubt, having one of his 'episodes'.

Darkus used his thumb to raise his father's closed lids and saw the pupils were indeed fixed and dilated. Wilbur whimpered in an effort to communicate, but Darkus took several moments to compose himself, waiting for his own heart rate to return to normal and his emotions to adjust to this new but not unexpected reality.

Darkus then reached in his pocket, took out his phone, and dialled.

Chapter 9
TAKING THE LEAD

Bogna genuflected and made the sign of the cross as paramedics attended to Knightley's unconscious but breathing body. Darkus stayed by his father's side, explaining the condition to the ambulance technician. Clearly, intense stress was the trigger for these narcoleptic trances – just as it had been in the past – but that didn't make them any less terrifying. Darkus informed the officers of the local Heath constabulary that he had witnessed an assault of some kind, but that he couldn't identify the assailant, except to say that he was male and massively built.

'Are there any signs of bite marks?' Darkus asked the technician.

'Not that I can see,' she replied, puzzled. 'Was there an animal involved?'

'I don't know.'

Darkus chose, for obvious reasons, not to inform them of the case he and his father had been working on, or the gruesome scene he'd witnessed in the clearing at the base of the hill. Whoever – Darkus avoided the temptation of calling it 'whatever' – had attacked his dad was certainly human in form, and was definitely a male; stealthy, physically adept and cunning as well. This was an intriguing and dangerous combination.

There was that word again: the *Combination*. Darkus avoided the urge to credit that shadowy organisation with recent events – although his father would certainly have been looking for that connection. The Combination did, after all, draw its membership from all walks of life, both criminals and law enforcement – perhaps even drawing from the paranormal as well.

For the time being, Uncle Bill was out of play, and the only person who could help identify the suspect was now in a trance – besides, his father's memory couldn't be relied upon at the best of times. Once again, Darkus was alone and facing a dark conspiracy beyond his comprehension. He consoled himself with the fact that his dad was in one piece and his vital signs were normal. The question remained: was Darkus equipped to continue the investigation on his own?

Wilbur watched, confused, as Knightley's body was stretchered to an ambulance waiting on one of the

Heath's access roads. Knightley was subsequently observed for a few hours at the Royal Free Hospital, before phone calls were received from a government department called SO 42 that none of the doctors or nurses had ever heard of. Then at 10 a.m. Knightley was loaded into a wheelchair and released into Bogna's care. She drove him straight home to Cherwell Place in the back of the Fairway cab, with Darkus and Wilbur in tow.

Darkus was relieved to find no dogs watching the office.

Bogna executed a fireman's lift and carried Knightley single-handedly up the stairs to his office, where she laid him in his customary position on the sofa, with a tartan blanket and a TV set up nearby. Feeling the need to be near him, Darkus took his dad's position at the desk, overlooking him. Wilbur quietly curled up at his young master's feet, exhausted.

Very aware that he was now alone, Darkus looked at his phone and scrolled to the name: *Tilly*. Being a Sunday, she would probably be preoccupied with something – an obscure bit of research or a new piece of software – but it seemed to make little difference to whether she picked up the phone or not. If she wanted to take a call, she took it; and if she didn't, a thousand calls would happily go unanswered.

After a few rings, Tilly picked up: 'I can't talk right now.'

'Are you at home?' asked Darkus.

'No . . . Are you?' she replied.

'No . . .' They both fell silent. 'Listen, I might need your help with something . . .'

'Look, I'd like to help, really I would, but it's not a good time.'

There was something odd in her voice. 'Not a good time?' said Darkus. 'But –'

'*Trust* me,' she said emphatically. 'I'll call you when I can.' She hung up.

Darkus stared at the phone for another few seconds, puzzled. What could she possibly be doing that was more important than the case he was currently facing?

Frustrated, Darkus switched screens to the photo album, flicking through the various images he'd collected during the eventful past twelve hours. The secure phone Uncle Bill had given him on their first assignment was equipped with editing functions that could enhance images to nearly retina quality – in other words, there were so many pixels in the image that the human eye couldn't tell the difference. It was almost as good as being there.

Darkus opened the photo of the large paw print, carefully examining the markings.

It was abnormal for several obvious reasons. The indentations were deep, indicating a large body mass, yet the claws were short and had barely made an impression. Secondly, the four cushioned pads of the paw were widely spread, yet the metacarpal pad, which usually sat just behind them for stability, was missing altogether.

Darkus glanced down at Wilbur's paws as the dog slept. As he suspected, the print from the Heath was something entirely new. As well as the metacarpal pad being missing, the carpal pad, which usually wouldn't make contact with the ground at all, had left a clear impression – meaning that the whole paw must have been held at an awkward, near-impossible angle.

Darkus committed these notes to his small black book, then took a deep breath and continued looking through the photo album, getting to the more horrifying images. He could never let these get into the hands of the unfortunate pets' owners. Whatever fate they had imagined for their loved ones, it could never have been as sinister and agonising as what had actually happened. He felt chills behind his neck as he observed the aftermath of the animal's ferocity. The staring eyes, or gaping sockets, the distorted jaws and limbs spreadeagled, all on display in this hideous, private gallery. But a gallery of whose making?

Darkus was interrupted by Bogna knocking and entering with a tray of sandwiches balanced on her forearm. He quickly clicked his phone off.

'I think you need some sandwich to keep you going,' she announced, pointing to each set of triangles in turn. 'I bring chickens livers, spam and gammons.'

'Thanks, Bogna, but I'm not hungry right now. I'll have them later.' Darkus winced, swallowed and smiled politely.

'Whatevers.' Bogna shrugged, set down the tray and closed the door behind her.

Knightley continued sleeping, his trance uninterrupted by the noise. Clearly he'd tried to protect Darkus from the true horror of what was taking place on the Heath. And despite Darkus's instinct to please his dad by solving the case, he knew it would be reckless to return to the scene of the crime without proper back-up.

Darkus willed his mind to move away from the gallery of images and on to the next problem. Who was the figure in the woods that had attacked his father? Was this massively built man the owner, or guardian, of some kind of predator that was hiding out there, using the sprawling urban wilderness as its own private game reserve? Using it for sport? After all, humans had been doing the same thing to animals since history began.

He looked at Bogna's tray of sandwiches and gagged a little.

Finding no obvious answer to the problem, Darkus sat back in his father's chair to clear his head. Wilbur quivered and jerked in his sleep, as if fighting off unseen enemies. Darkus quietly watched him, respecting the principle of letting sleeping dogs lie, and realised that despite losing his father to a state of unconsciousness again, he had gained a four-legged partner. Whatever Bogna had unlocked in the mutt had resulted in Wilbur becoming an almost functional police dog again. Yes, Wilbur didn't respond to commands as promptly as he could have done; and yes, when faced with a truly scary scene, Wilbur had turned tail and run away. But most of those poor deceased souls were his canine brethren, so who could blame him? And when Darkus whistled, Wilbur most definitely came.

Feeling his curiosity piqued, Darkus remembered something Captain Reed had said at the dog rescue centre. Darkus picked up his phone again and typed a search into the internet browser: *war dogs*.

He tapped on a link and began reading.

War dogs dated back to as early as 600 BC and had been used by armies throughout history, from the Greeks and the Romans, to the Americans in Vietnam and the allies in modern-day Iraq. The dogs often wore armour: more recently that meant Kevlar vests to repel bullets and shrapnel, but hundreds of years ago they would have worn chain mail and spiked collars. In the early days they accompanied the horsemen as they entered battle, running ahead to break the ranks of the enemy. During the Middle Ages, war dogs were given as gifts between royalty, so they could breed their own lines of canine soldiers. During World War One, a former stray Boston terrier named Stubby became the first dog to be promoted to the rank of sergeant. Sergeant Stubby was shot at, gassed, and reportedly even managed to capture a German spy by the seat of the man's trousers. The mutt, who had begun his career as a stowaway, proved invaluable in the trenches of France, using his exceptional sense of smell and hearing to warn his unit of mustard gas attacks and incoming artillery shells. Despite being wounded in the foreleg, Sergeant Stubby recovered and was soon back in the trenches, before returning home to a hero's welcome in the United States. He spent the twilight of his life as a mascot at American Football games where he would routinely dribble the ball around at half-time. After what any dog would consider a full and active life – if a short one – he passed away at the age of around nine or ten. Being a stray, there was no birthdate on record.

Darkus suspected there was a line of war dogs in Wilbur's ancestry – but did that make his job easier or not? Darkus was the third generation in a line of private detectives, after his father of course, and his father's father, Rexford. The line may have extended longer for all he knew. It was in Darkus's blood and he could feel it, but that didn't make his chosen career any less challenging, or the sacrifices he had to make any less painful. Both Wilbur and Darkus had had their childhood denied them, because it was just preparation for their true calling, which would engulf them and make other concerns seem petty. Perhaps that's why they seemed to understand each other so well. Even when Wilbur was at his most difficult, there was a bond there that couldn't be broken. Besides, since leaving Wolseley Close, the dog appeared to be going from strength to strength, rediscovering both his skills and his confidence.

Darkus continued browsing, finding accounts of US soldiers from the ill-fated military intervention in

Vietnam in the 1960s and 1970s. Veterans from the war described how their dogs kept them company on night patrols and saved their lives countless times by sniffing out explosives. They could even detect snipers by the smell of gun oil from their rifles. Spending twenty-four hours a day under constant threat of death, the dogs and their handlers built a relationship that was stronger and more enduring than any other relationship in the soldiers' lives. Wives and girlfriends may leave them, families may forget about them, but the dogs would never leave their side. The handlers learned to talk to them, to strategise and plan their operations, even if they didn't receive a verbal response. It helped the soldiers keep their heads and in some cases to keep their sanity. The dogs had been trained to respond with basic movements, like coming to a halt and sitting down to indicate an explosive in the area; or biting the soldier's hand if he was about to touch a tripwire.

It was estimated that war dogs saved the lives of ten thousand men in Vietnam.

Darkus kept seeing the same phrases repeated over and over again: '*He helped me get back in one piece, physically, and mentally.*' '*He was my best friend.*' '*They did everything for you.*' '*They gave so much, and expected so little . . .*'

Tragically, when the Vietnam War came to an end, the generals gave orders, and the remaining soldiers were evacuated, but their beloved dogs were not. Approximately five thousand dogs served in Vietnam, but only two hundred dogs returned home. The remainder were either put to sleep, or left behind. Some soldiers even tried to extend their combat tours to remain with their dogs. In quote after quote, Darkus saw the familiar heartbreak again: *'Leaving my dog was the hardest thing I ever had to do . . . These dogs knew more about honour, duty and devotion than most people today.'* There were still soldiers, decades on, who couldn't even talk about their dogs. It still bothered them.

Darkus clicked on a war dog memorial page that contained the names of all those missing or lost in action, along with the K-9 promise from dog to soldier:

> *'My eyes are your eyes, to watch and protect.*
> *My ears are your ears, to hear in the dark.*
> *My nose is your nose, to sense the enemy.*
> *And as long as you live, my life is yours.'*

Darkus looked down at Wilbur and decided for once to break the rule of letting sleeping dogs lie. He knelt beside the German shepherd and gently gave him a hug. Wilbur started for a moment, before he settled back down and rested his head on the carpet, returning to whatever dreams or nightmares he was having.

Darkus took a shower and freshened up, partly to wash away the memory of the hanging room; and partly to erase any remaining scent that might prove useful to his enemies – whether they were real or supernatural.

When he returned to his father's office, he found Knightley Senior still unconscious, just as he'd left him, but Wilbur was sitting in the corner of the room, cowering with his tail between his legs. The tray of sandwiches was strangely empty.

'You must have been hungry.'

Wilbur twitched his light brown eyebrows apologetically.

It was noon and Darkus realised nature would soon be calling on Wilbur, so he picked up the lead and the Metropolitan Police Kong toy, ready for their walk, hoping the fresh air would provide a solution to the facts. Wilbur bounced up and wagged his tail repeatedly across Knightley's face.

But Knightley just kept sleeping.

Chapter 10
THE SCENT OF THE CRIME

Darkus walked Wilbur along Cherwell Place, looking over his shoulder to check that they weren't being followed, either by pedestrian, car or canine; then they proceeded up the crowded high street. The swell of humanity faced Wilbur with a fresh set of challenges. Each new scent appeared to tempt and confuse him. Darkus noticed the dog was having trouble walking in a straight line, as every sensation lured him in a different direction. Darkus deduced that it must have been a while since Wilbur was on active duty around the general public.

Darkus decided to steer off down a side street, before they found their way to Highbury Fields, a tree-lined park in the centre of a residential neighbourhood, where a mix of young and old peppered the grass.

As Darkus and Wilbur crossed the park they encountered a variety of canines: some were finely coiffed

117

lapdogs, others were pit bull terriers bred for violence and street status, following orders from their young masters, who appeared equally aggressive under hooded tops. Darkus remembered a phrase from his earlier canine research: '*It travels up and down the lead. If you're confident, the dog is confident.*' Darkus straightened up and walked on, undaunted. Wilbur, in turn, appeared unfazed, inspecting the pit bulls with professional disdain. Darkus observed this, feeling inwardly proud, and tried to adopt the same approach with the owners.

Darkus found a secluded area of grass and let Wilbur off the lead. He took the Kong toy and threw it as far as he could. Wilbur galloped after it excitedly, before turning back with the toy in his mouth, wagging his tail in a frenzy. Wilbur ran back and delivered the Kong into Darkus's gloved hands, then jumped up and rested his paws on his master's chest gratefully.

'Don't mention it,' said Darkus, laughing.

For a moment, they were just an ordinary boy and an ordinary dog.

Wilbur hopped down and rolled on the grass, wriggling and scratching his back, then flopping over and playing dead.

'You're a terrible actor,' said Darkus, smiling. 'Here . . .'

He prepared to throw the toy again, until Wilbur sat

up and began barking at something behind him, with a curious mixture of apprehension and excitement.

Before Darkus could turn around, a voice answered, 'It's OK, Wilbur.'

Wilbur sat down obediently. Then another voice followed it:

'Sorry tae interrupt ye tway's playtime . . .'

Darkus turned to see the corduroy-clad bulk of Uncle Bill limping across the park towards them. He was accompanied by Captain Reed from the rescue centre, wearing grey army fatigues and a raincoat.

Darkus instinctively went to stand by Wilbur's side.

'Don't worry,' said Reed, 'we're not here to take him away.'

Wilbur bounded towards the captain's side, greeting his former master.

'Quite the opposite as it happens,' added Bill, removing his homburg hat and shifting from his bad leg to his good one. 'Ah convinced the docs tae let me return tae work. Just packed Dougal aff tae his forsaken lighthouse.'

'How did you find us?' demanded Darkus.

'Bogna told us ye were oot for a walkie. The rest was deduction. Simples,' he said with a smile.

Darkus noticed Uncle Bill's Ford saloon parked off at the edge of the grass.

'That still doesn't explain what you want with us . . . Here, boy,' Darkus instructed Wilbur, who obediently returned to him and sat.

'He's coming along well,' said Reed.

'What can I do for you gentlemen?' asked Darkus.

Bill looked at Reed for a moment, then back to Darkus.

'We have a wee problem that I think ye Knightleys might be able tae assist us with,' Bill began.

'Dad's had another episode,' said Darkus defensively.

'Ah'm aware of that, Doc.'

'And I suppose it's just coincidence that you're here making your proposal in his absence? So he can't object? Just like on the last case.'

Bill shrugged, impressed with the boy's guile. 'This is of vital importance tae the department – any one of their lives could be in danger at the next full moon,' he warned grimly.

'Dad was right,' said Darkus. 'There *is* something on the Heath. I'm not prepared to say that it's supernatural, but it's definitely . . .' he paused, looked for the right word, 'highly antisocial.'

'We have more tae worry aboot than missing pets, Doc. London appears tae be crawling with strange canines, and they're hunting down *mah* men. I've had tway of them watching mah hoose.'

120

'Me too,' replied Darkus.

'I will nae say *what* they are, but they're crafty as hell. They're fast, they move too quick tae follow and they rarely leave any evidence behind. If they dae, it's left as a sign, as if tae say, "We know where ye live." However, with the right support, we believe ye and Wilbur here might be able tae help us find oot where they live, what they want, and who their keeper is. Before the next full moon of course. That's in less than seventy-tway hours.'

Darkus thought it over.

'We had a verra successful collaboration on the last case, ye must admit,' Bill pleaded.

'Help you how?' said Darkus.

Bill rummaged in his voluminous overcoat before pulling out a plastic evidence bag containing a small fragment of torn corduroy.

'This wee bit of trooser belonged tae one of the intended victims. Tae *me*, as a matter of fact. It's coated in dried dog's saliva. Disgusting,' he explained. 'They recovered it on the Millennium Bridge after mah wee high dive. It's been kept tightly sealed since then, so the scent does nae escape.' He waggled the evidence bag in the air before them. 'I believe with the right nose on the job, this may lead us tae the perpetrator.'

'You expect us to follow *that*, across the whole of London, maybe beyond?'

Captain Reed flipped up the collar of his raincoat and chimed in, 'Wilbur here was attached to the bomb squad and special operations. He has a very unique set of skills. When we can't detect things, and machines can't detect things, we have to rely on a superior sense.' Reed nodded towards Wilbur. 'When it comes to counterterrorism, the K-9s are our last line of defence.'

Darkus looked down at his dog, confused.

'Wilbur,' Reed almost barked. 'Find the gun,' he instructed.

Darkus stood back as Wilbur reared up on two legs and appeared to paw at Uncle Bill's overcoat.

'Ho ye!' Bill exclaimed, chuckling as Wilbur nuzzled into his armpit and pulled out a small snub-nosed revolver.

Wilbur then sat down and dropped the gun on the grass.

'Good boy,' said the captain in clipped tones.

'Well, that was a tad overfamiliar,' said Bill, straightening his clothes, embarrassed. 'May ah pick up the mahaska?' Bill asked Reed. 'Mah piece?' he implored.

'Give,' ordered Reed, then Wilbur retrieved the gun and dropped it in the captain's hand. Reed balanced it in his palm before passing it back to Bill. 'Odd weight for a .38.'

'Aye, that's because she's loaded wi' silver bullets,' replied Bill, matter-of-factly. 'Ah'm nae taking onie chances.'

Darkus raised his eyebrows.

Reed continued. 'Wilbur can detect gun oil at several hundred metres, among many other danger signs.'

Darkus watched Wilbur anxiously. 'I still don't see how he could possibly trace a scent across an entire city.'

'We've scoured the CCTV cameras at the scene of the crimes,' Bill went on. 'The dogs are always alone, with nae owner in sight. They always return tae the north side of the river. By comparing the footage of the dogs we've narrowed down their last known where-aboots tae a one-square-mile radius aroond Victoria Train Station. We believe that's enough to give ye and Wilbur a fighting chance of finding their HQ.'

Darkus thought it over, suddenly wishing for an ordinary life, and an ordinary walk with his ordinary dog.

'Why Wilbur? Why me?'

'He's got the snout, ye've got the brain. The Knightley brain. With the Knowledge on board too. That's a dynamite combo.'

Darkus didn't look convinced.

'A'right, Darkus, it's like this,' Bill went on. 'If they see me or Cap'n Reed, the game's up . . . Besides,' he confessed guiltily, 'nae one suspects a child.'

'What if they already suspect me? They've been to Wolseley Close.'

Bill pouted and shifted on his feet.

'What you mean is,' Darkus concluded, 'I'm deniable.'

'There's nae denying it. Nae.'

As usual, Darkus didn't really understand what the Scotsman was saying – and he got the impression Bill liked it that way.

Fortunately for Bill, Darkus had the bit between his teeth and wasn't about to let go.

'With the right support,' granted Darkus, 'we may be of assistance.'

'I cannae guarantee a surveillance drone or an armoured battalion, Doc. The department is facing greater austerity measures than ever. Even my meal allowance is in jeopardy. But ye have mah word I shall oversee the operation personally.'

Darkus considered his position. Nothing about the operation sounded appealing, other than to see what Wilbur was really capable of, and to prove once again to his father that he was a worthy business partner – and maybe, just maybe, to get to the bottom of what had put his dad back in a trance. Besides, as long as the 'smart' dogs were watching them, they'd never be truly safe.

The question was, were Darkus and Wilbur 'smart' enough to catch them?

Chapter 11
THE HUNT

Less than an hour later, Darkus watched London through the window of the Ford saloon, finding himself compressed in the back seat with Uncle Bill on one side and Wilbur on the other. Reed sat up front next to the driver, who Darkus recognised from their last assignment. Wilbur's window was cracked open for him to sniff the air, his jowls leaving a residue of slobber on the glass.

Before departing, Darkus had assembled his customary tools of the trade: his phone, fingerprint kit and a jeweller's loupe (a small cylindrical lens which served as a miniature magnifying glass). Bogna had assured him that his father would be well taken care of in the usual way, and sent Darkus and Wilbur off with a packed lunch – although Darkus was unsure which sandwiches were for him and which were for the dog. As the catastrophiser hummed insistently at the back of his head, he was reminded that there was still one critical element missing. And that was his stepsister, Tilly.

She would bring that X-factor that Darkus couldn't provide: her knowledge of the street, of emotions and human behaviour, which could not be learned in books no matter how many hours one spent reading. While Darkus was confident in his encyclopaedic knowledge of detective work, Tilly had an encyclopaedic knowledge of what makes people tick: the fine strings that make up someone's personality and how to tug on the right one, to play them like a harp. Darkus suspected he would never understand people the way he understood cases.

Darkus stared at his phone keypad. Should he call her again? She'd already mentioned she wasn't at home – that meant both of them were on the loose at the same time. In due course this would attract unwanted attention from Clive, the school authorities, or maybe even social services.

What was she doing anyway? Perhaps she was more preoccupied with the mysterious hoodie on the motor scooter who'd courted her in the early hours outside Wolseley Close? Darkus reminded himself that Tilly was still a wild card and could not be relied upon as an operational certainty. Yes, she had helped him recover his father on the last case, but not before risking life and limb in her own dogged pursuit of the Combination.

She had her own agenda and it was jaded by tragedy: to track down those members of the Combination who were responsible for her mother's death. If Darkus's mission deviated from that agenda, he could *not* count on Tilly to be there in a crisis – or even to pick up the phone. And if he was honest with himself, Darkus couldn't blame her. She was more alone than he had ever been. She was damaged, badly – but Darkus hoped not beyond repair.

Darkus put his phone back in his pocket and familiarised himself with his surroundings. The saloon pulled out of the plodding traffic and parked illegally by the kerb of Terminus Place, opposite the main entrance to Victoria Train Station. Uncle Bill strained to open the car door and hoisted himself out.

'Follaw me,' he bellowed.

Bill led Darkus, Wilbur and Captain Reed away from the Ford saloon as it briskly accelerated back into traffic. Darkus looked up at the once grand façade of Victoria Station, which was now encroached upon by the road barriers of London's busiest bus terminal. A large clock occupied the centre of the station's frontage, keeping time as legions of travellers hurried beneath it.

Bill led them through the bustle of people and queuing red buses to a white Transit van parked strategically across from the station entrance. The van had a ladder strapped to its roof and a builder behind the wheel with his feet on the dashboard, reading a tabloid newspaper. Darkus recognised the set-up from his last assignment: that particular operation had resulted in an attempted assault, a frenzied foot chase and the prime suspect being flattened by a bus. Hopefully this time round the going would be easier – although Darkus wasn't convinced it would be and the catastrophiser was skittering in the background, making all the wrong noises.

Captain Reed climbed into the centre seat beside the driver, then instructed Wilbur to jump up next to him. Reed closed the door and wound down the window, then Bill passed him the evidence bag containing the torn piece of corduroy. The captain whispered something in Wilbur's ear, then opened up the plastic to deliver the scent. Wilbur poked his snout right inside the bag, burrowing around, as if hunting for an invisible snack. He drew in the smell and allowed the molecules to be processed by the two hundred and twenty million nerve endings that make up the canine nose – as opposed to the mere five million in the human one.

Darkus reluctantly left Wilbur at the passenger window and followed Uncle Bill through the back door of the van. Inside was the customary array of TV monitors and surveillance equipment, with the familiar lanky male technician at the keyboard. Bill slumped into a wheelie chair, which threatened to career off towards the door, until he dug his heels in and scooted over to the monitors, replacing his hat with a telephone headset.

'A'right nou, Wilbur is going tae sit up front and see if he can catch a whiff of the suspects. Captain Reed, can ye hear us?' Bill spoke into his headset.

'Wilbur and I are primed and ready,' Reed answered through the mic from the front seat.

'What happens if he gets the scent?' Darkus asked Bill.

'We're tapped intae the London Transport cameras, here, here . . . and here.' Bill appeared to get confused. 'And here.' He massaged his bald pate and continued. 'Once we have a visual on the beasties I want ye and Wilbur to follow at a safe distance. If ye lose visual for a moment or tway, dinna worry, Wilbur will pick up the scent again. See where they go, who they associate with, find oot anything ye can. And we'll be following ye on the cameras and tracking ye with yer phone . . .' Bill handed Darkus a small flesh-coloured earpiece. 'Every move ye make, we'll be watchin' ye . . .' he intoned in his Highland burr.

'Sounds like nothing could go wrong,' said Darkus, not without irony.

'Aye. Naething whatsoever,' Bill assured him.

Darkus took a deep breath, pulled up a wheelie chair and watched the array of CCTV images splashed across the monitors. People flowed in all directions like human estuaries running in and out of the main body of the train station. Darkus forced his mind to ignore the people and only look out for the animals. He lowered his field of vision to the pavements and walkways. Hidden here and there were poodles, lapdogs, the occasional guide dog, and the very occasional stray cat.

Bill sat back in his chair and tore open a large packet of chocolate biscuits.

'Would ye care for a bicky?' he offered. 'I find they help tae pass the time.'

'Thanks.' Darkus accepted one and took a bite.

Bill took another two for himself, forming a makeshift sandwich, which he slid into his mouth in one go. 'Have ye ever tried them frozen?' he said, blowing a fine spray of biscuit crumbs over the desk. 'Locks in the taste, gives 'em that extra bite,' he explained like a connoisseur.

Time seemed to elongate and expand as they watched the monitors. Rain showers and sunbursts came and went. The movement of images across the screens resembled a procession of clouds across a horizon. The people blurred into one, multiplying then contracting, breaking, reforming, then diffusing. All on their way to their own particular destination, with their own agenda.

Darkus rubbed his eyes as they entered the second hour of viewing. The sun had begun to drop in the sky and pointed shadows were extending over the canopy and walkways at the front of the station, giving the CCTV images a bluish tinge as the cameras' infrared light systems flicked on to defeat the darkness. The footage reflected across the technician's glasses and over Bill's smooth head, which had lost balance and was now propped at an unnatural angle. Darkus realised Bill was either asleep or in a food coma.

The only sound from the front seat was the occasional whimper, followed by Reed explaining, 'Negative. It's nothing.'

Darkus remained focused on the screens, mentally noting each fleeting animal appearance in the crowd, until . . .

'Wait –' Darkus said, peering closer at one particular camera angle. 'There . . .'

The technician captured the image then enlarged it, making a high-pitched beeping noise, which roused Bill from his slumber.

'Aye! What is it, Doc?'

'That looks like one of the dogs.' Darkus pointed at the screen.

A Rottweiler mix trotted purposefully between the legs of a dense crowd of travellers at a pedestrian crossing, heading towards the main entrance. The dog appeared to be untethered, but moved too stealthily for bystanders to notice it. It weaved through the foot traffic towards a youth in a hooded top, waiting on the pavement, holding a white stick.

'It's just a guide dog,' said Bill, poking his finger at the screen as the youth in the hooded top patted the dog, then followed it into the main entrance, pointing with the white stick.

They were interrupted by a loud *woof* from the front seat. Reed's voice followed it through the headset:

'Wilbur's got something.'

'Look at his stride,' said Darkus in quick staccato, staring at the youth. 'He doesn't look blind.'

Darkus moved closer to the screen, seeing a *second* youth in a hooded top, also holding a white stick. A *second* identical Rottweiler mix emerged from the crowd and led the youth into the station.

'Since when have they used Rottweilers as guide dogs . . . ?' Darkus whispered to himself.

'Since never,' said the technician and switched to a different camera angle as the two youths entered the terminal and began making their way across the packed concourse.

'Gae, gae, gae,' Bill instructed Darkus, while banging on the wall of the van.

Darkus hopped out of the back of the white van to

find Reed and Wilbur waiting for him on the pavement. Wilbur was now wearing a black, Kevlar-lined tactical vest. Reed handed Darkus the lead. Darkus wrapped it round his wrist and patted Wilbur nervously.

'Remember: your eyes are my eyes,' Darkus whispered. 'Ready, boy?'

'Find them,' Reed ordered, and Wilbur immediately tugged on the lead, pulling Darkus across a congested bus lane towards the station entrance.

Darkus had to run to keep up as Wilbur dodged through the tight knot of travellers, causing him to knock people out of their path.

'Hey, watch it!' a pedestrian called after them.

'Sorry –' Darkus muttered in response and continued after Wilbur who appeared to be locked on to the scent.

Darkus adjusted his flesh-coloured earpiece as Bill's voice blurted through it: 'Aye, Doc, we have ye in our sights. The tway bogies are heading for the platforms with the beasties in tow.'

Darkus followed Wilbur under the canopy and through two ornate stone arches into the main concourse, which was overrun with signage and dotted with shops. The enormity of the task became clear as Darkus saw hundreds of travellers moving in all directions, almost colliding with each other as they walked towards their respective platforms.

Wilbur stood with his back perfectly arched, his head upright and legs evenly positioned. He bobbed his nose left and right, discerning between the thousands – if not millions – of smells in the train station. The aroma of coffee and pastries in one direction, burgers grilling in another. Wilbur's nostrils flared and narrowed repeatedly as he drank in the scene, but he wasn't eager for food, he was only looking for the one scent that mattered.

'I don't have a visual,' Darkus said to himself, knowing Bill would hear him through the earpiece.

'Wait a second,' Bill's voice announced as he observed the cameras. 'They're getting something tae eat. The little bleeders. It looks like . . . yes, it's a Cornish pasty! Go tae the Pasty Shop at platform nine.'

Darkus looked past the giant departure boards, ignoring the flickering orange letters, and instead looked for signs to the platforms.

At that moment, Wilbur tugged him forward at a sprint, having found the scent. Darkus stumbled after him through the melee of train goers.

'Haud on. They're heading yer way!' Bill warned Darkus through the earpiece.

Wilbur accelerated again as the thick crowd parted briefly to reveal the two hoodies holding white sticks, their pale white faces obscured under baseball caps. The

Rottweilers marched at their sides in a perfectly matching half-step, then suddenly came to a halt.

Both hounds raised their noses to the air, detecting trouble.

Wilbur also came to a halt, nervously assessing his opponents.

Darkus remembered the phrase: '*It travels up and down the lead. If you're confident, the dog is confident.*' He stood his ground as the crowd rejoined around them, blocking the hoodies' view. But the hounds had the scent.

The Rottweilers abruptly sat down on the spot, causing the hoodies to stop dead and look at each other, realising something was wrong.

At just that moment, the crowds parted again to reveal Darkus and Wilbur standing a scant thirty metres away from the suspects.

Both Rottweilers raised their jowls and their thin black lips rolled back to reveal matching rows of perfectly symmetrical and impossibly sharp teeth. Instead of growling or barking, they emitted a series of excited, rhythmic grunts – as if eagerly anticipating what was about to happen.

The two hoodies glanced around, noting the CCTV cameras angled at various locations on the walls and roofs of nearby shops. Calculating that this was not the place for a stand-off, the hoodies both whistled sharply and darted off in the direction of the exit with the Rottweilers on either side of them.

'They're on the move,' Bill's voice blurted.

'I can see that,' Darkus replied as Wilbur yanked his arm and gave chase.

Wilbur slalomed through pedestrians, dragging Darkus with him.

The hoodies ran towards the exit, then banked left and deviated into the corner of the station under a blue sign that read: *Victoria Underground Station*. They sprinted down a set of stairs, knocking bystanders out of the way, the dogs racing beside them in perfect time.

'They're going for the Choobe!' Bill's voice erupted. 'Don't lose 'em!'

'I'm doing my best –'

Darkus bobbed and weaved after Wilbur as they ran at full pelt down the stairway to the Underground. Pedestrians were by this time moving to the handrails to make room as the three dogs and their owners blazed a trail through the Tube station.

Darkus jumped the last few stairs to the ticketing area and saw the hoodies and their dogs jump one after the other over the barriers, in perfect unison, then continue on towards the platforms. A pair of police officers ran towards the scene but were instantly taken down by the two Rottweilers who wrestled them to the ground, tearing their yellow visibility jackets and threatening to rip them limb from limb. The officers screamed in help-less terror as the hoodies kept running. After a few seconds the dogs left their prey like limp rag dolls and sped after their handlers.

Wilbur accelerated after them, breaking free of Darkus's grip and hurdling the ticket barriers. Darkus saw more police officers converging on the scene and stayed calm, removed his Oyster card from his pocket, swiped the machine, passed legally through the ticket barrier, then sprinted after Wilbur.

The hoodies reached the platforms, breathless, just as a District Line train arrived. The dogs looked about, their nostrils flaring and stubby tails wagging furiously, having the time of their lives. The hoodies pushed and antagonised their way through the waiting travellers to reach the front of the line. The Tube train came to a stop and the automatic doors slid open.

Darkus caught up with Wilbur and picked up his lead.

'Doc, I'm losing ye . . .' Bill's voice screeched and broke up into digital interference.

Wilbur barked in the direction of the train, causing bystanders to back away, making a circle around him and Darkus. As the deluge of people parted again, Darkus saw the hoodies and their dogs board the train and begin shoving their way through the carriage.

The automatic doors began to slide closed until . . .

Darkus placed his foot in the way, causing the doors to stutter and slide open again. Darkus and Wilbur squeezed on board. The doors slid shut and the train jerked into motion. Wilbur barked, grabbed the lead in his jaws and passed it to his master, shaking it violently. Darkus understood. 'OK, boy. Be careful –'

He unclipped the lead from Wilbur's collar and the dog set off through the moving train, burrowing through the travellers' legs to follow the scent.

Darkus ploughed through the passengers after him, until a burly man stepped in front of them to block their way.

'What d'you think this is – ?' he blathered.

The man was interrupted as Wilbur leaped up and took him to the floor. Darkus stepped over the stunned man and continued.

Up ahead, the Rottweilers picked up speed, reaching the door connecting the carriages. Incredibly, the lead dog reared back on its hind legs, then used its paw to depress the metal handle and open the door, allowing them through. The handlers followed suit, swiftly closing the door behind them. It was clear the dogs were the true masters and the hoodies were just following orders. The hounds forged ahead, snapping at anything and everything in their path, leaving a trail of chaos in their wake.

The Tube quickly arrived at Sloane Square station. Wilbur and Darkus were still one carriage behind. The doors slid open and Darkus craned his neck to scan the platform for the dogs, but they appeared to have stayed on board. Affluent couples carrying shopping bags added to the train's load, finding themselves pressed against each other as the doors slid shut behind them. The hoodies jostled with the shoppers, kicking bags out of the way, finding their progress slowed, giving Wilbur and Darkus time to catch up. The hoodies pushed through the next set of doors, persistently making their way towards the other end with Wilbur close behind.

Travellers yelled and moved to either side of the carriages, crushing the seated passengers as Darkus and Wilbur found themselves in a straight-line pursuit of the suspects down the length of the train.

The dogs galloped through the narrow space, knocking bags and belongings in all directions. Darkus picked his way through the debris, trying to keep up.

The hoodies reached the front of the train and turned back to see Wilbur closing the gap, ready to attack. The Rottweilers stomped and chattered, salivating and wagging their tails in anticipation of a fight, but the hoodies appeared to be following prearranged contingency plans. One of them reached into his jacket, pulled out a crowbar and wrenched open the train driver's door. The hoodies and their dogs barged into the cabin and overpowered the driver. One hoodie pulled a knife and held it to the man's neck, while the other used the crowbar to jam the door closed.

Wilbur leaped at the door but it easily withstood his assault and he bounced off it and collapsed in a heap. Wilbur scrabbled back to his feet as Darkus arrived beside him.

'What do we do now?'

Inside the cabin, the hoodies flanked the driver, with the knife still jabbing against his neck.

'Drive,' said one of them.

'I can't. We're approaching the station –' the driver faltered.

'I said *drive*.'

The driver's eyes went wide as he sat rigid in his seat. The speedometer kept a steady fifty-five miles per hour. The cabin started to beep as instructions burst through the intercom demanding that he stop.

'Say nothing,' warned the hoodie.

The dogs stood poised, steady as rocks as the Tube train careered along the tracks and sped through South Kensington station.

Waiting travellers were virtually thrown back across the platform by the force of the train as it barrelled through the station without stopping. Within seconds it had exited the tunnel at the other end.

Inside the cabin, the hoodies laughed to themselves at the sight of the shocked bystanders recoiling away from the train. In the carriages behind them, passengers began to protest and soon after to scream.

'Faster,' urged the hoodie.

The driver didn't argue, he just cranked it up. 'There are trains in front of us. What if – ?'

'We'll take that chance,' the other hoodie replied. 'You'll stop when *I* tell you to.'

The train tore through Gloucester Road station, sending waiting travellers scattering in the same fashion. The hoodies laughed again.

Outside the cabin door, Darkus looked at the passengers wailing in fear, then called out to them: 'Hold on!'

He reached up for the emergency stop handle and pulled hard. For a moment, nothing happened. The passengers looked at each other in confusion.

In the cabin, an override option started beeping rapidly.

'What's that?' demanded the hoodie.

The driver didn't answer.

'Tell me or I'll bleed you dry . . .'

The driver waited another second, then said, 'It's too late now –'

The emergency brakes automatically activated, gripping the rails and showering the undercarriage with sparks as the entire train decelerated rapidly.

In the carriages, passengers hurtled forward, cartwheeling over each other. The deafening scream of metal grinding on metal made the scene inside the train resemble a silent but catastrophic mime show. A hail of sparks flew past the windows, lighting up the tunnel. Bags slid across the floor as if magnetically attracted to the front of the train. Darkus and Wilbur were slammed against the locked cabin door, then fell to the ground, stunned.

Inside the cabin, the hoodies were thrown against the windscreen of the train, which cracked but didn't shatter. The dogs stood perfectly balanced, remaining upright the whole time. Only their ears twitched as the Tube train ground to a squealing, shuddering halt, with a noise like nails on a blackboard. They were now stranded between stations. The driver tried to leap from his seat until one of the hoodies punched him to the floor, while the other stepped on his unconscious body, held on to a pair of handles and swung his legs, ferociously kicking out the windscreen. The Rottweilers immediately jumped through the hole in the cabin and ran down the middle of the tracks in the beam of the stationary train's headlights. The hoodies clambered out and jogged along behind them.

In the carriage, Darkus reached for his hat and replaced it on his head, feeling a fresh bruise developing under the brim. He watched as an automatic door obligingly slid open with a hiss, then he and Wilbur hopped out on to the side of the tracks beside the wounded train. Somewhere an alarm bleated, echoing through the tunnels. What was it about him and the Underground, Darkus thought to himself. He realised with some consolation that the trains on the District Line would be stopped as a matter of protocol. This meant he could continue the pursuit on foot without fear of being mowed down – for now. Of course the hoodies must have known this as well. It was all part of their escape plan.

The hoodies and the dogs had turned a corner in the tunnel, deserting the glare of the train's headlights. Wilbur sniffed around and found the scent again, trotting down the middle of the tracks after them. Darkus went into the darkness behind him. He checked his earpiece and patted down his pockets for the secure phone – but they were *missing*. They must have fallen out during the emergency stop. He silently cursed. Wilbur turned the corner of the tunnel and Darkus realised it was too late to go back. Uncle Bill would have to follow *their* trail now.

Darkus jogged after Wilbur as he saw the beams of several torchlights dancing off the walls some three hundred metres up the tunnel. Then he heard the growl and bark of the Rottweilers and the terrified screams of what Darkus deduced were London Underground maintenance workers who'd had the misfortune of crossing paths with them. The torchlights fell to the ground, their beams pointing in all directions. Darkus caught up with Wilbur as he sniffed the workers' sprawled bodies. Darkus checked their pulses: they were alive, but in a severe state of shock.

Confirming that none of the victims needed immediate attention, Darkus followed Wilbur as he continued down the tracks, past emergency lanterns that hung from the pipes and cables lining the inside of the tunnel. Wilbur pursued the scent without deviation. They passed openings in the walls that offered glimpses of parallel Tube lines, all converging on a surface station, which was now visible, lit by the last rays of daylight at the far end of the tunnel. The emergency lanterns were replaced by red, white and blue London Transport signs, bearing the words: *Earl's Court*. The tunnel suddenly opened on to a large, lit platform area sheltered by an iron canopy.

Darkus caught sight of the Rottweilers effortlessly leaping up from the tracks on to the platform, with the hoodies dragging themselves up after them. A small circle of bystanders gathered to witness the scene.

Wilbur paused, summoning his energy, before springing up after them, scrabbling with his back legs as his front paws failed to gain purchase on the platform surface. He managed to haul himself up in a haphazard display, before looking down, concerned, at Darkus, who tossed his hat up to him. Wilbur duly caught it, then watched as Darkus pulled himself on to the platform after him.

The crowd of bystanders watched in amazement as the German shepherd in the tactical vest passed Darkus his hat, then the pair set off up the stairs after the Rottweilers. Darkus had lost visual contact, but Wilbur followed the scent like a heat-seeking missile, through the busy transport hub to the Warwick Road exit. Emergency workers in high visibility clothing ran in the opposite direction, heading for the stricken District Line train. Darkus followed Wilbur through another set of turnstiles, swiping his Oyster card and coming face-to-face with the curving art deco façade of Earl's Court Exhibition Centre. Darkus looked down to see Wilbur already darting across traffic to reach the opposite pavement.

'Wilbur! Wait –'

Darkus gave chase, dodging oncoming vehicles. Three hundred metres down the busy thoroughfare, he saw the stubby end of a Rottweiler tail turning the corner into an adjacent street. Moments later, Wilbur and Darkus arrived at the intersection, panting and hyperventilating.

'Where are they . . . ?'

The adjacent street was empty except for a few pedestrians. Then Darkus saw two stubby tails turn another corner off in the distance, as if leading them deeper into a maze.

In seconds, Wilbur and Darkus arrived at the next intersection to find a row of shops and houses – but still no dogs.

Darkus surveyed his surroundings. Darkness was falling. Wilbur raised his snout to the air and bobbed it about. Then the dog reluctantly proceeded down the street, more hesitant this time.

'What's wrong, boy?' Darkus asked.

Wilbur shook his head as if he was shaking off water.

'What is it?'

Wilbur sat down on the spot – to indicate danger.

Darkus came level with him and looked ahead down the road. Nothing appeared out of the ordinary. A series of shops led past a small housing estate with a tall block of flats looming overhead. But once again, Darkus was relying on the visual and sonic spectrums, whereas Wilbur was attuned to the olfactory one: in other words, *smell*.

Darkus suddenly detected a familiar and pleasant aroma. It was the smell of freshly brewed coffee, and appeared to be wafting across the entire area. Yet there was no café or coffee house in view.

Darkus sniffed again, surprised at how pungent it was, then looked down at Wilbur and realised: it was a smokescreen. Or in this case, a smell-screen. It was the same trick that drug traffickers used to outwit sniffer dogs – simply conceal the illicit substance in coffee granules.

The smell of coffee was obscuring the Rottweilers' scent.

Wilbur whimpered, frustrated. Darkus glanced up at the tower block again and saw curtains twitch on two separate floors near the summit. Was it his imagination, or were he and Wilbur being watched? And where was that pungent coffee odour coming from?

'It's OK, boy,' said Darkus. 'We'll just follow the coffee.'

Darkus clipped the lead to Wilbur's collar and they carried on across the road and into the housing estate.

They descended a concrete path lined with metal railings, past a row of well-kept garages and a cluster of smaller blocks of flats, which encircled the imposing high-rise. Two dim, fluorescent street lamps provided the only light. Now equally equipped – with Wilbur's senses having been dulled by the coffee – Darkus led the way into a wide recreation area with a deserted playground in its centre. Strangely, there appeared to be no one in the entire estate.

Darkus scanned the symmetrical rows of balconies, doors and windows, none of which exhibited any sign of life. Then he noticed something odd. Thin plumes of steam were rising from dozens of windows that had been left slightly ajar around the estate.

This was where the coffee smell was coming from.

Darkus counted approximately twenty-five windows dotted across the various buildings. Then he caught a glimpse of something else. Wilbur stood on his hind legs, seeing the same thing . . .

The two Rottweilers trotted across a long communal balcony near the top of the high-rise block. There was no sign of their handlers. Darkus quickly calculated that the suspects were ten storeys up. The canines continued along the open corridor and approached a red door at the end of the tenth floor, nudged it open with their snouts and entered.

Darkus squinted, confused. Wilbur panted, returning his front paws to the ground, unsure how to proceed. Darkus waited a full thirty seconds, before cautiously wrapping the looped leather handle of the lead around his hand and approaching the high-rise. CCTV cameras were angled on them from various vantage points – but it was unclear for whose benefit the events were being recorded. The catastrophiser oscillated nervously, telling Darkus that something bad lurked inside. The hairs on the back of his neck stood on end in an almost animal reflex.

Darkus and Wilbur walked up a dimly lit walkway and pushed through a heavy set of doors into a dark entrance hall. Two rows of overhead bulbs led to a pair of polished steel lift doors. Darkus pressed the call button and the doors opened, revealing a clean, empty lift car waiting for them. Wilbur sniffed around, then reluctantly followed Darkus inside. Darkus pressed the button for the tenth floor, the doors closed and the lift gently ascended.

Moments later, the doors opened on to the long, communal balcony that connected the flats. Darkus ventured out, now overwhelmed by the smell of coffee still wafting through the air, even at this height. Wilbur shook his head violently, trying to shake the smell out of his nostrils, but the odour wouldn't budge.

They walked along the deserted balcony, past rows of louvred glass, towards the red door at the end of the corridor. Darkus got a start as an elderly female resident looked up from her kitchen counter as they passed her window. Darkus smiled, but she avoided his gaze and returned her attention to a large saucepan on the hob, full of what appeared to be coffee bubbling. So there were people here, he reasoned. But why did they appear to be confined to their homes? And who was instructing them to create this caffeine smokescreen?

Wilbur strained at the lead, not wishing to go any further. Darkus patted him on the head and urged him along. They passed three more residents, aged from thirty to sixty, all of whom appeared equally surprised and apprehensive to see them. All of whom avoided eye contact and returned to making coffee. Darkus led Wilbur on, arriving at the red door, then knelt down to examine it. The door was slightly ajar, and no lock appeared to be engaged. Darkus slowly pushed the door open and prepared to enter, until . . .

Wilbur bit down on Darkus's hand, drawing blood.

'Ouch – !'

Darkus clutched his wounded hand and looked up at Wilbur in shock. Wilbur sat down on the spot, unapologetic. Darkus followed the dog's gaze to a tiny, gleaming metal filament crossing the doorway at waist height.

It was a tripwire.

Darkus hovered over the wire, realising how close he'd come to some kind of surprise attack – and how Wilbur was the only one who could have prevented it. He nodded gratefully to the mutt who remained sitting, implacable.

Darkus took off his hat, lowered himself to the floor and carefully slid through the doorway on his front in a commando crawl, keeping the tripwire a few centimetres above his head. Wilbur followed suit, shuffling his paws along the ground to duck underneath it.

'Wait –' Darkus whispered, calling a halt himself this time.

He angled his head to see the metal filament that crossed the doorway was hooked up to an improvised pulley system, which was connected to a long, thick, tension cable, which was connected to a spring-loaded mechanism, which was part of a lethal-looking contraption on the linoleum floor just inside the doorway. The device was over a metre in length and consisted of two long rows of rusted, metal teeth, like a dog's jaws yawning open in wait. It resembled a relic from a medieval torture chamber.

Darkus realised, with a sick feeling in his stomach, that it was a *mantrap*.

Darkus slid past the jagged machine, being scrupulous not to let any part of his body or clothing come in contact with the finely tuned spring. Wilbur continued to crawl behind him, exercising the same caution, as they cleared the perilous doorway and entered the flat.

Darkus rolled on to his back on the linoleum and checked his immediate surroundings. There was a bathroom on their left, a kitchen to their right, and a living room ahead of them. The curtains were drawn at the windows, with only a few chinks of neon peering though.

There was one further door, which was closed tight, but contained a ring of artificial light around the frame. Darkus looked to Wilbur for any signals. Wilbur raised himself up and pointed his nose at the closed door. Darkus silently got to his feet, keeping his eyes peeled for any further threats. Then he very slowly reached for the door handle, turning it in infinitesimal degrees, until the latch disengaged and the door opened.

What met his eyes next was even more unexpected.

Chapter 12
ALL HAIL THE KING

The door opened into what at first appeared to be a vast, white space. Darkus thought a spotlight must be shining straight into his eyes, until he realised that the gaping whiteness was not a starry illusion created by his visual cortex. It was *real*.

The door opened not into a room but into a brightly lit cavern. Wilbur sat close by his side, refusing to budge. Not quite believing his eyes, Darkus looked down and discovered a set of metal steps descending below the level of the flat he'd just exited and leading into what looked like a dungeon of some kind. The structure of the building was still intact but the dividing walls and floors had been stripped down to bare iron girders and pipes, hollowing out a large chamber in the middle of the high-rise block. Pulleys and cables ran along the beams, carrying platforms and lights. A concrete screed extended across the floor. The impression was one of a theatre set that could be rearranged at will. In keeping with that impression was the cast of characters who awaited Darkus on the chamber floor.

It was a modern-day Fagin's lair. Some twenty youths of indeterminate age and ethnicity were assembled in the centre of the space, all with hoodies pulled up and drawstrings fastened to conceal their identities. Some were masked as well. The two Rottweilers, along with another four identical dogs, were standing perfectly poised, flanking a truly astonishing figure who dominated the front row. He was well over six feet tall, somewhere in his late forties, wearing a quilted nylon waistcoat and a white button-down shirt, ripped jeans and trainers – all of which barely seemed able to accommodate his massive frame. His shoulders hunched aggressively around a cluster of muscles that made up his neck. His chest expanded with each quick breath and his biceps visibly flexed under the shirt, resolving into thick forearms and huge hands. He appeared to be an animal only partially contained in human form.

His face was not obscured. He clearly felt no need to disguise himself. His cranium resembled a piece of chiselled granite, his shaved head and massive brow overpowered a pair of darkly shining eyes with unusually small irises, a straight nose, an angular jaw and a thin, cruel mouth.

Darkus's catastrophiser whirled and he turned back up the stairs, but the door of the flat slammed shut, trapping them in this hellhole. The six Rottweilers silently bared their teeth at Wilbur, saliva dripping from their gurning mouths. Wilbur stuck close to his master as they descended from a sort of gallery, ringed with floodlights, which illuminated their reception committee.

'Allow me to introduce myself,' the figure said in a deep monotone. 'I'm Barabas King.'

Darkus recognised the name from the Knowledge. *Barabas King.* He began flicking through the contents of his mind to locate the relevant information. He felt adrenalin flood his system, raising his heart rate, leaving him jittery but numb. He tried to remain calm and plucked up enough courage to open his mouth. 'Are you telling me because you intend to kill me?'

'I'm telling you because you probably already know,' King replied dismissively. 'Your reputation precedes you, Master Knightley.'

Darkus nodded, finding the relevant file in his head, then reciting from it: 'Notorious London crime boss. Your father was unknown. Your mother tragically died during childbirth. You spent time in and out of prison your whole life – not to mention several psychiatric institutions. As I recall you were sectioned under the

Mental Health Act for the best part of a decade. It would seem their work was not successful.'

King shrugged his huge shoulders, listening to his biography. 'Please. Go on.'

'Despite repeated allegations of extortion, blackmail and murder, you haven't had a single conviction in the last nine years,' Darkus went on. 'Nothing would stick. "Teflon" is the modern parlance. You're even rumoured to have filed down your own teeth to strike terror into your opponents –'

King smiled, his lips curling open to reveal a set of razor-sharp teeth, like dagger points. 'You've done your homework,' he snarled.

Darkus swallowed hard. 'The question is . . . what are you doing with a pack of highly trained dogs? And who's *your* master?'

'I don't answer to anyone,' he replied, his voice tinged with violence.

King looked at one of the hoodies, then nodded in the direction of a window high on the opposite wall. The hoodie pulled a cable, which raised a shade to reveal a view of a modern glass-fronted skyscraper located only a few streets away. The building was brightly lit, its offices all populated, even after hours.

'You see how close that is?' King asked. 'That's the Empress State Building. Home to close to a thousand

Metropolitan Police officers. But d'you think any of them ever stray on to my turf?' He laughed twice, like the sharp double tap of an automatic weapon. 'Never. They're too afraid of what might happen to them. It's the law of the jungle over here. People get *eaten*.'

Darkus made a mental note of that last sentence. 'And I suppose it's no coincidence,' he remarked, pointing at the Rottweilers, 'that dogs matching their description have been tracking and murdering senior police officers during the full moon.'

'Cry "Havoc!" and let slip the dogs of war . . .' King said theatrically.

'*Julius Caesar*, Act Three, Scene One,' Darkus replied. 'But this isn't Shakespeare.'

'But it *is* war,' King continued. 'This city has declared war on a whole breed of us. They're trying to wipe us out, but they won't use guns or knives. That's far too messy. They use money and influence. Councils, bureaucrats and property magnates.' He spread his rippling, muscled arms like a pair of wings. 'Do you know why I've torn the heart out of this building . . . ?'

Darkus studied the galleries and ropes disguised among the innards of the building, then shook his head.

'Because it's already tagged for demolition,' King purred. 'Every building in a one-mile radius . . . history.

157

It's going to be a playground for the rich, bought and paid for by foreign money. No one's going to live here,' he spat. 'This city's looking to stamp us out.'

'What's that got to do with killing police officers?'

'You take something of mine, I take something of yours. It's survival of the fittest. Not the smartest.'

The last comment appeared to be aimed at Darkus personally, but Darkus wasn't buying it. 'They're *not ordinary* police officers,' he went on. 'They're members of the Department of the Unexplained. An elite branch of Scotland Yard.'

'Your point being?' said King.

'Are more officers going to be targeted at the next full moon?' Darkus demanded, before going further. 'Are you working for an organisation known as . . . the Combination?'

'I sell my services to the highest bidder. What do the authorities expect?' King sneered at the Empress State Building through the window. 'They want a city with no residents? A city with all the lights off?' He smiled, exposing his pointed teeth. 'I'll make the most of the dark.'

Darkus examined his enemy closely. 'My dad believes there's a werewolf loose in London. On Hampstead Heath, to be precise.'

'Your father has a wild and unbridled imagination,' King replied.

'No offence, but they don't really look that friendly,' Darkus responded.

King smiled, then turned to his dogs. 'Dinner!'

The Rottweilers lunged forward, their paws clawing at the concrete, gaining traction as they raced across the floor towards Darkus and Wilbur, until . . .

King snapped his fingers loudly and all six dogs skidded to a halt obediently, waiting for instruction.

'You see, they're very good dogs,' King said proudly, then turned to address the canines. 'Eat *slowly*. It'll be more enjoyable . . .'

Darkus felt his bowels loosen and a chill run down his spine. He looked wide-eyed at Tilly, who looked as alarmed as he did. King raised his hand to give the command to eat – then stopped.

The six Rottweilers had all sat down on the spot and were staring in the direction of the window. King followed their gaze. Outside a single siren could be heard approaching the building, casting a blue light across the chamber. It was followed by a second siren and a third. A murmur travelled through the assembly.

King barked orders quickly. 'Dogs, heel!' The Rottweilers raced to his side and sat in formation. He pointed to Darkus and Wilbur, then turned to the hoodies. 'Get 'em out of here! Form a perimeter.'

A pair of lift doors slid open at the end of the room.

Darkus and Wilbur were grabbed and manhandled into a waiting lift car, flanked by hoodies. Wilbur barked at their assailants until Darkus brought him to heel.

'Not yet, boy, we're outnumbered.'

The lift descended smoothly with the hoodies jostling each other for position. Darkus found Tilly pressed in next to him, with Doyle beside her.

'You shouldn't have come here,' Doyle muttered. 'You're not one of us, you're one of them.'

'He's right,' added Tilly, as she quietly slipped Doyle's phone back into his hoodie pocket without him seeing.

'I'm sorry you feel that way,' Darkus responded.

'Today you live,' warned Doyle. 'But tomorrow you'll pay.'

The lift doors opened on to the entrance hall, revealing a row of police cars waiting in the driveway with Uncle Bill in the centre.

Doyle tightened the drawstrings of his hoodie to obscure his face, then shoved Darkus out towards the waiting police presence.

Both Darkus and Doyle turned to look for Tilly, but she'd vanished.

The hoodies formed a protective vanguard around the entrance as Uncle Bill approached, taking the cigar from his mouth and tossing it to the tarmac, stubbing it out with his orthopaedic loafer for effect.

'A'right, huiddies.' His words had no effect. 'Move along, ye hear?'

The youths didn't move an inch. The rest of the police officers appeared too afraid to intervene. Darkus approached the line of cars.

'Ye a'right, Darkus?' said Bill with concern.

Darkus nodded. 'Just about.'

'I smell coffee,' said Bill, intrigued. 'D'ye think it's for us?' His face brightened. 'D'ye think they'll have biscuits?'

'They're using it to disguise their scent,' Darkus replied flatly.

'Ay course, I knew tha', I knew tha',' blustered Bill.

'The real villain is inside,' explained Darkus. 'Wait here, boy,' he told Wilbur, who obediently went to Captain Reed's side.

'Lead on,' said Bill, then addressed the hoodies. 'Come on, break it up, break it up –'

Bill forced his way through the centre of the line-up, stepping on toes and scuffing trainers. Darkus followed in his wake, the way a car might follow the path of a snowplough.

Darkus walked ahead to the lift and stabbed the call button. The polished steel doors opened again and they stepped inside. Darkus pressed the button for the top floor.

Moments later, they were walking along the communal balcony towards the red door at the end of the row. The various residents looked up from their kitchen counters as Uncle Bill doffed his hat and flashed his badge at each in turn. Bill arrived at the red door, rapped on it and reached for the handle.

'Be careful –' warned Darkus, getting there first.

He knelt down low and nudged it open – then fell back as a miniature schnauzer raced to the door and began yapping furiously.

'Shut up!' an elderly man's voice yelled at the dog. Footsteps followed it to the door, which was pulled open to reveal a seventy-year-old man in a bathrobe and slippers. 'Can I help you?'

Darkus got to his feet, puzzled.

'Ye sure this is the right one?' Bill asked him. Darkus nodded. 'We have a warrant,' Bill went on, trying to uncrumple a piece of paper.

'Be my guest,' said the old man and ushered them in.

Darkus walked straight to the left-hand door and opened it, expecting to find the set of stairs descending into the chamber – but instead he found an elderly lady, with her feet on an ottoman, watching TV. Darkus ran his hand along the walls, which were adorned with ageing paintings and built in cupboards. He tapped on each one but the construction felt solid. There was no sign of any secret chamber whatsoever.

Darkus examined the faces of the elderly couple, but they were either completely unaware, vaguely senile, or professional actors. Concluding that any one of these theories was equally plausible, but equally impossible to prove, Darkus realised he'd been outplayed.

He turned to Bill. 'I was held hostage by the crime boss, Barabas King . . . right here in this room. In a chamber below this room to be precise.'

Uncle Bill fumbled for his walkie-talkie. 'A'right all units, search the entire building.'

'He'll be long gone by now,' said Darkus, perplexed.

'Well, whadd'ye suggest we dae?' enquired Bill.

'I don't know,' Darkus replied frankly. 'But King's out for blood and we've only got two days until the next full moon.'

Brendan Doyle watched Darkus and the police officers return to their cars empty-handed. The rest of the hoodies disbanded and walked into the darkness or re-entered the building. The motorcade of cars exited the estate and the streets cleared out. Brendan found himself all alone as he walked across the recreation area to his waiting motor scooter. He picked up the black carbon helmet with the devil's horns on either side of the visor, fished for his keys and turned the ignition.

He climbed aboard and gunned the engine, which sputtered and whined. He folded the kickstand and pushed away, cruising around the playground and towards the exit.

Then he applied the brakes, finding that a metal gate had been lowered to block his path. He shrugged, turned the wheel and motored across to the other side, then came to a halt, finding the same thing.

'What the – ?'

He turned the wheel and did a U-turn to find the two hoodies from Victoria Station standing before him, flanked by the two Rottweilers.

'You called the 5-0,' the first hoodie said.

'What?! Who?' Doyle asked, genuinely confused.

The dogs' eyes shone and glittered in the night.

'The police, the Special Branch,' the second hoodie said. 'You called 'em.'

'I don't know what you're talking about!' Doyle shouted.

'Then *someone* used *your* phone.'

'That's impossi–' He pulled out his phone to check his recent calls, then saw an unfamiliar number and did a double take. 'There must be a mistake.'

'We don't allow mistakes.'

166

The hoodies whistled and the Rottweilers took off across the tarmac.

Doyle cranked the throttle and sped across the recreation area, bouncing up and down on the seat, nearly losing control of the back wheel. The scooter weaved and wobbled away from the running dogs.

The Rottweilers caught up with unnatural speed, snapping at the rear licence plate and pulling it off. Doyle cranked the throttle again, doing a wheelie as he crossed on to a pedestrian walkway, which was his only means of escape. Doyle grinned, getting the upper hand as the dogs' speed was impeded by the incline.

Doyle half flew over the brow of the walkway and on to the flat part leading to the main road. All that stood in his way now was a set of metal barriers to prevent vehicles such as his using the pedestrian path. Doyle realised, even with his skill, he would not be able to guide the scooter through this tight set of railings. He turned back to see the dogs gallop over the crest of the hill, leaving a fine spray of spit and steam in their wake. Doyle revved up, wheelied on to the narrow parapet that ran above the path and accelerated along it, bypassing the barriers. His wheels were only just slim enough to stay on solid ground. Like a fairground performer he kept his balance as the scooter traversed the low wall and bounced back on to the path with a crunch, arriving at the main road.

He raised his fist in triumph. 'Sick!!!'

Then the scooter lurched and decelerated with a clattering sound as the exhaust pipe dropped off and trailed along the road. The engine spluttered and complained, losing speed.

'No – !' The exhaust drowned him out.

Doyle went pale inside his helmet and cranked his head to see the Rottweilers leap straight over the barriers and zero in on him. He urged the scooter on, rocking back and forth, willing it forward. The Rottweilers leaped again in perfect synchronicity . . .

The scooter toppled and smashed to the ground, its rear wheel spinning fruitlessly in space. The engine ran free with a high-pitched scream – which went some way towards hiding the human one.

Doyle struggled helplessly on his back. The black helmet with the horns was tossed aside as the beasts smothered the rider on the ground. A few curtains twitched in the windows of the high-rise overhead, then were still.

Chapter 13
A WAKE-UP CALL

Darkus sat in the back seat of the Ford saloon with Wilbur while Uncle Bill took the front seat next to the driver. Captain Reed had made his apologies and returned to the rescue centre where his other dogs required attention. Bill had given Darkus a new secure phone to replace the one that was lost in the tunnel – clearly the mission wasn't over yet.

Wilbur wouldn't sit still and kept circling on the seat, sniffing around in the footwell below it, until the driver took a sharp turn and a small yelp escaped from the heavy tartan blanket at their feet. Darkus looked down as the fabric unfurled to reveal Tilly curled in a ball under the seat. Wilbur wagged his tail and made room, pleased to see her.

'Nice of you to drop in,' said Darkus. 'You were a big help back there,' he added with a hint of sarcasm.

'Why d'you think the boydem showed up when they did, huh?' Tilly snapped.

'By "boydem" are ye referring to *me*?' asked Bill, a little insulted.

'I believe it's current street parlance for the law enforcement community,' Darkus explained.

'And what the hell were you doing there in the first place?!' she challenged him, dragging herself up on to the back seat. 'You nearly compromised a two-month, deep cover operation.'

'Doing what?' said Darkus. 'Maybe if you were more willing to share information, we might build a new spirit of cooperation.'

'Whatever. You were lucky I was there at all,' she replied. 'I had to borrow Brendan's mobile in case they'd bugged mine.'

'So that's what you were doing on the back of that scooter. Hanging out with Doyle.'

'I don't expect you to understand the importance of field work. You can't learn everything from books.'

'I can't see what you'd learn from the likes of *him*.'

'That sounds like jealousy in your voice, Darkus. It doesn't take a great detective to spot that. Brendan isn't so bad really. His parents are lawyers, so yeah, he tries a bit hard to be all gangsta – but he can take care of himself, and he took care of me. And he knows people who know people, and they all work for one person: Barabas King. And King is so big I'm betting he's connected to the biggest baddie of all: and that's *the Combination.*'

Darkus knew she could be right, but it was too early to entertain that possibility without proof, and it felt too much like something his father would say. 'You're as bad as my dad,' he said. 'There's no hard evidence that the Combination's behind this. King's too insane to be kept on a leash by the likes of Morton Underwood or his colleagues – that's if Underwood's even alive. Besides, King said it himself: he answers to no one.'

'You really think he'd admit to anything in front of his band of artful dodgers? Or that he'd have access to the kind of resources necessary to send highly trained dogs to whack senior police officers?'

'How d'ye know about tha'?' said Bill from the front seat.

'I read the news, I question the official story. All you need is a computer, an internet connection, a natural curiosity and an ability to blend in.'

Darkus nodded. He couldn't help being impressed by Tilly's ingenuity.

'And guess what?' Tilly went on. 'It's no coincidence that each of the victims lost a small article of clothing in the lead-up to the full moon.'

Darkus turned to Bill. 'Is this true?'

'Now ye say it, I did lose a glove a few days befoore mah attack.'

Darkus caught on. 'They used it as bait for the dogs. To give them the scent.'

'Precisely,' said Tilly. 'Of course there could also be an occult connection. I'm not excluding anything at this point.'

'It had a Custard Cream hidden in it tae,' muttered Bill. 'Lucky bleeders.'

'I'd prefer to deal in the rational,' said Darkus. 'This sort of thing was common practice in East Germany during the Cold War. The secret police kept thousands of pieces of fabric in jars, taken covertly from potential dissidents, in order to track them with sniffer dogs at rallies or insurrections.' He closed his encyclopaedic brain for a moment. 'But that doesn't bring us any closer to stopping King. Or to finding out who's going to be targeted at the next full moon.'

They were interrupted by the bagpipe ringtone of Bill's secure phone. He patted himself down, locating the phone in a commodious inside pocket.

'Aye,' he said into the handset. 'Aye, aye, aye.' He relayed the information to Darkus. 'Nae sign of King. Nae sign of the beasties. The building's clean.' He listened again. 'Aye . . . Ew . . . OK.' He hung up, then turned to face Tilly. 'I'm afraid it appears yer mucker Brendan Doyle was involved in a particularly . . . *nasty* hit-and-run accident.'

'No –' Tilly stammered. 'Is he dead?'

'He's been admitted tae hospital with what they're calling "life-changing injuries".'

Tilly looked down, biting her lip until blood trickled down one side of her mouth. It was closely followed by a stream of bitter, stinging tears. 'I have to see him.'

Bill shook his head. 'He's under police guard. Nae one's getting through.'

She looked up at Darkus, her mascara running. 'He was covering for me. Because he liked me . . .'

Darkus reached over and held her around the shoulders, reluctantly, because he didn't know the rules for this sort of engagement, but he instinctively knew it was what she needed. 'It's not your fault . . .'

'I should've known,' she insisted.

'We're not dealing with ordinary criminals.'

'You're right,' she sobbed, pushing him away, then wiping off the mascara in a horizontal smear that resembled warpaint. 'They take people's lives away, without mercy. Like they took away Mum. And that's why they're going to *pay*.'

Darkus had to remind himself that few of Tilly's reactions would ever be as calibrated or rational as his own.

The Combination had murdered her mother in a freak car 'accident', and no matter how much anyone tried to make up for that loss, those scars would never heal. And due to the fact that her mother had been his father's former assistant, deep down Darkus knew Tilly would always hold him and his dad responsible too.

The Ford saloon pulled up outside 27 Cherwell Place, then Darkus, Tilly and Uncle Bill approached the blue door with Wilbur in tow.

Bogna greeted them each in turn, reserving an extra big hug for Uncle Bill who appeared to lift her clean out of her Crocs for a few seconds.

'Och, yoo're a big lassie . . .'

'Mr Billochs, really.' Bogna blushed under her housecoat. Then she pointed Wilbur in the direction of a bowl of what appeared to be cabbage stew, which he wasted no time in consuming hungrily.

Darkus led the procession to his father's office, where Knightley remained composed but unconscious on the sofa, with the Discovery Channel playing on TV.

'How is he?' Darkus asked.

'Nothing changes,' said Bogna. 'He say somethings during his bed bath, I don't understand what . . . You want I make some sandwich? Triangle not square?'

Darkus and Tilly nodded gratefully.

'That'd be stoatin', Boggers,' Bill replied eagerly.

Bogna smiled coquettishly, straightened her apron and vanished downstairs.

Darkus relayed the details of his pursuit and subsequent capture at the hands of Barabas King, then Tilly provided supporting information on his gang and their methods of operation. Bill listened, awkwardly shifting his weight in the armchair and intermittently wheezing.

'King could be hidden in any number of estates across London,' Tilly explained. 'He's impossible to track. I've tried.'

'What about the dogs?' asked Bill. 'How's he training 'em? And why are the attacks happening at the full moon?'

'Murderers have a habit of striking on significant dates,' said Darkus. 'From serial killers to terror groups. They often pick dates that are numerologically or culturally significant. As well as describing the date September 11th, the numbers 9-11 are also the phone number for the US emergency services. Perhaps that was no coincidence.'

Tilly nodded. 'Superstition adds to the sense of terror, which is exactly what King wants. To frighten his opponents into submission.'

Darkus turned the evidence over in his mind. 'The full moon is the perfect decoy. Everyone's chasing werewolves, while the real culprits are perfectly ordinary attack dogs.'

'Wait a second,' Tilly interrupted. 'There's nothing ordinary about those dogs. Whoever's behind this has trained them to track their enemies like laser-guided missiles. That could only be the work of a state-sponsored group. Or a group large enough to draw on multiple assets – perhaps even the supernatural.'

'You're talking about the Combination again.'

'It's the only answer,' said Tilly bluntly. 'And remember, those dogs were sniffing around *your* house and *your* office.' She gestured to the Knightleys' head-quarters. 'I'll put money on *you* or your *dad* being next.' She looked around. 'By the way . . . where's your hat?'

Darkus checked around, before realising with a sinking feeling. 'I left it at the tower block.'

'Whit da – ?' Bill anxiously searched about for his own hat, then realised it was still on his head.

'Coincidence . . . ?' Tilly asked Darkus. 'I think not. Looks like you need my help. Again.'

Darkus checked his watch, then turned to Tilly. 'When is your dad going to notice you've gone AWOL?'

'He doesn't seem that bothered any more. He still gets memory lapses,' she explained. 'Must be the aftermath of Underwood's post-hypnotic suggestion. Sometimes he doesn't seem to know I'm there at all.'

'What about Mum?'

'Jackie? She's more concerned about *you*,' Tilly said with a trace of envy, then shrugged. 'I figure I can stay out until the full moon. That's only two days from now.'

'I'm aware of that,' said Darkus grimly.

The door pushed open and Wilbur entered, followed by Bogna carrying a tray of sandwiches. As Bogna gave detailed descriptions of each one, Wilbur curled up at Darkus's feet. Darkus realised he'd missed the quiet companionship of his four-legged friend, who seemed a world away from the war dog he'd witnessed in action a few hours earlier. Now slumped at his feet, without the tactical vest, the German shepherd was just like any other household pet: a lovable furball, someone to confide in, who would silently understand without passing judgement. For a person who thrived on exchanging ideas and competing theories, this was a calming antidote for Darkus. Talking to a pet might seem like a safe option, or a captive audience; after all, Wilbur would never open his mouth to question his judgement – although he'd done just that during the pursuit. Yet, for Darkus, confiding in someone who couldn't talk back was second nature. That was the state his father had been in for those four long years – and was in again now.

Knightley's chest heaved and fell as Bill and Tilly helped themselves to the sandwiches, but Darkus had lost his appetite.

Bogna fetched Tilly a self-inflating mattress and some blankets, making up a bed for her on the landing. Uncle Bill said his goodbyes and returned to the Ford saloon which was waiting outside. Darkus remained in the armchair with Wilbur at his feet, watching his father. Tilly soon fell asleep beyond the doorway. The TV continued playing the Discovery Channel at a low volume. Before long, Darkus and Wilbur were asleep as well.

By midnight, the terraced house was vibrating with snores.

In the office, the Discovery Channel showed footage of a leopard chasing a gazelle across the African tundra. A sober narrator explained: 'The *combination* of speed and agility gives the wild cat an effortless advantage over its hapless prey . . .'

From the sofa, Knightley's hand clenched into a fist, then his lips began to curl into a malformed word. 'Cohmm . . . bin . . . ation . . .' he mumbled quietly. The word appeared to be waking him up, just as it had done with his last 'episode'. Then he went quiet again, his hand falling limp, in the same position as before.

The other investigators were none the wiser.

Outside the house, a lone figure arrived on Cherwell Place, her slim figure casting a thin shadow over the pavement. She paused as two Rottweilers exited the street at the other end, strangely trotting side by side. She cocked her head and adjusted her trilby hat as she watched their stubby tails turn the corner. She waited warily for a moment, then headed towards number 27, unshouldered her leather reporter bag, reached under the flap of her belted raincoat and dug in her trouser pocket, pulling out some small change. She chose a one-pence coin, reached back and hurled it up at the top window. It plinked against the glass, almost hard enough to break it, but fortunately not quite. The coin skittered away into the road.

Darkus woke with a start as Wilbur raced to the window and balanced his front paws on the ledge. Tilly and Knightley continued snoring, apparently unperturbed.

Darkus rose from the armchair, parted the curtains and peered out, seeing the female figure on the street below. He hesitated, waiting until he had a positive identification, then closed the curtains and guided Wilbur to his basket.

'Stay here, boy. Don't wake anyone up.'

Darkus pulled on his herringbone coat and crept across the landing.

He descended the stairs, hearing the bronchial rumblings from Bogna's quarters, then opened the front door and walked past the railings to the street. The female figure sauntered to greet him.

'Sorry to drop in on you like this,' she said.

'Hello, Alexis,' said Darkus cautiously. 'What can I do for you? Not another photo shoot I hope? I haven't had my beauty sleep.'

Alexis smiled, resting one foot on the pavement and exposing a slender trouser leg through the folds of her raincoat.

'I've got all the shots I need. And like I said, you can call me Lex.' She curled a lock of blonde hair under her hat and waited for him to respond.

'So, what can I do for you . . . Lex?'

She reached in her reporter bag and pulled out a freshly printed newspaper, bearing the name: *The Cranston Star*.

'I wanted you to see tomorrow's headline,' she said proudly and handed him the paper.

Darkus unfolded it to reveal the front page:

EXCLUSIVE: What is stalking Hampstead Heath?

Darkus felt the colour drain from his face as he began to read:

Detective duo Knightley & Son are investigating bizarre events at the North London beauty spot following the unexplained disappearance of dozens of animals, amid reports that a dangerous predator is on the loose. Some are even speculating it's a 'werewolf'. Veteran private eye Alan Knightley is believed to have fallen back into a narcoleptic trance, leaving Cranston's own Darkus Knightley leading the investigation . . .

A photo of Darkus, covertly taken, filled the lower half of the page. Inset was a photo of the Tai Chi man.

'What have you done?' he whispered.

'It's called investigative journalism. This is my big break,' she boasted.

Darkus felt his blood begin to boil, at the same time as his eyes were blinded by her charms. His heart and mind had declared war on each other.

'You'll jeopardise the whole investigation,' he warned. 'You might even jeopardise *lives*.'

'I'm hoping for national coverage on this one. Anyway, I wanted you to be the first to know.'

'Is there anything I can say or do to stop you?' Darkus pleaded.

She looked him over, sizing him up. 'Sorry, Doc, but this is bigger than both of us.' She shrugged and slung her reporter bag over her shoulder, before delivering a parting shot. 'Guess I'll see you when you get back to school, whenever that is.'

She walked off into the darkness, leaving Darkus alone clutching the newspaper.

Chapter 14
STRICT CONFIDENCE

When Darkus finally got himself back to sleep, just before dawn, it was a plunge so deep into the unconscious that a number of things happened around him that he was completely unaware of. Upon waking, it took him several moments to realise that he was no longer dreaming. Tilly *had* materialised at the council estate the previous night and rejoined him as a partner in crime-solving. Alexis *had* arrived on Cherwell Place in the early hours and delivered a copy of *The Cranston Star*, which remained protectively rolled up under Darkus's arm, and which – much to his frustration – threatened to blow the whole investigation wide open. But most staggering of all, when Darkus opened his eyes and adjusted to the daylight, he found that his father was no longer lying unconscious on the sofa, and in fact the sound of his animated voice was clearly echoing up the staircase from the living room.

Darkus looked around, noticing that Tilly's mattress had been folded away and Wilbur's basket was empty. He checked his watch: it was nearly eleven o' clock. Finding it hard to fathom how he'd slept so late, he struggled to his feet and thudded down the stairs.

Bogna was mopping the hallway when she looked up and saw him.

'Master Doc. Alan is awake! They are having a meetings.'

She pointed the dripping mop head at the living-room door, where a large pair of Hunter wellie boots had been propped outside.

'They are?' Darkus asked, feeling oddly left out. Why had no one taken a moment to wake him? And who were they meeting?

Darkus turned the door handle and walked in to find a bizarre parlour tableau of characters. His father sat in an armchair with his feet on an ottoman, fully dressed and looking, it must be said, better than ever. Wilbur sat perfectly upright by his side, with Tilly next to him on the carpet with her legs crossed. A golden retriever was inexplicably curled up by the fireplace, watching the proceedings.

'Good morning, Doc,' said his father. 'Nice of you to join us.'

'I must have overslept . . .' Darkus said, confused.

184

'You might say I did too!' quipped Knightley. 'But for some reason I woke up right as rain. We allowed you some extra shut-eye to keep you fresh for the investigation.'

'Dad, I need to talk to you. Urgently –'

Knightley held up his hand to shush him. 'First, say hello to our distinguished guest . . .'

Another figure looked up from the armchair facing the fireplace. Darkus instantly recognised her as Fiona Connelly, the larger-than-life presenter of *Bad Dog*.

'Doc, you remember Miss Connelly,' Knightley announced.

Darkus wasn't certain if he'd woken up – the whole scene had the strange quality of a dream.

'Hello again, Doc,' she replied in her dainty but strict upper-class tone, which resembled that of a headmistress at an all-girls school.

Without the dogs for cover, her physique was even more buxom than before. Her white hair was tied up in a bun, hovering over large-framed granny spectacles and a slash of red lipstick. Her figure offered great rolling hills of country tweed; her jacket looked like it might split open at any moment, barely able to accommodate her pneumatic bust. Her tree-trunk thighs were compressed into a thick woollen skirt with an oversized, decorative safety pin to guard her dignity and keep the folds closed. Judging by her sturdy, stockinged calves and double-socked feet, the Hunter wellies could only have belonged to her. All of this was completed with a sweet perfume that reminded Darkus of Victoria sponge cake. Wilbur must have concurred because he sat happily silent, his nostrils slightly raised to drink in the aroma.

Dazed, Darkus answered awkwardly. 'It's an honour, Miss Connelly. I see you've met my dog, Wilbur.'

'Yes indeed,' replied Fiona. 'He's a gorgeous fella, aren't you, Wilbur.'

Wilbur wagged his tail cheerily.

'*Good* dog,' she cooed by way of a reward.

'You may remember, Fiona mentioned a problem she needed assistance with,' Knightley explained. 'Upon waking from my slumbers, I got straight in touch, and, well, you'll see that it's a most curious and unusual case.'

Darkus continued to listen, mystified.

'I take my security very seriously,' Fiona went on. 'So on your father's advice I came over at once,' she added.

Darkus looked to Tilly for some kind of affirmation. Tilly just shrugged and nodded, confirming that this was someone to be believed.

'So to business . . .' Fiona announced. 'I propose to hire Knightley and Son to investigate an intruder on my property. The following conversation must of course be held in strict confidence.'

'Confidence is our middle name,' replied Knightley. 'As you know, we charge a reasonable flat rate per day, regardless of the client. Plus expenses of course.'

'Very well,' Fiona agreed.

'Proceed,' said Darkus.

'Being a public figure, and a woman living alone,' she explained with a slight blush and a vigorous straightening of her jacket, 'I find it necessary to protect myself and my family.'

'I thought you said you lived alone,' Darkus interjected.

'My furry family,' she replied, gesturing to her golden retriever, as if it ought to be obvious.

'I see,' said Darkus.

'As well as hosting a successful TV programme about dogs, I am also a dog-lover. Perhaps, I am told, that is why I, myself, am still . . . unattached. And very much . . . available.' She glanced at Knightley, whose eyes went wide, before he covered himself with an innocent smile. 'For that reason,' Fiona went on, 'I have had installed at my home a state-of-the-art alarm and surveillance system. It is able to detect intruders and alert me of their presence. It is also able to display any visitors on a series of CCTV cameras that are linked back to my flat screen TV or iPad.'

'I am aware of such systems,' said Darkus. Tilly nodded, indicating that she was as well. 'Do you live in a particularly high crime area?'

'Not particularly, no,' Fiona replied.

'If you don't mind, where is your property located, Miss Connelly?' asked Darkus, building a case history in his head.

'Overlooking Hampstead Heath,' she answered.

Darkus looked to his father, who raised his eyebrows in a silent acknowledgement.

'I see,' Darkus continued, suddenly more interested. 'And as you have the benefit of 24-7 surveillance cameras, might I ask why you haven't been able to identify this intruder already?'

'Because it's not a person,' Fiona responded, looking pale. 'It's an *animal* of some kind.'

Darkus, his father and Tilly all exchanged a glance.

'Please describe it for me,' Darkus said, reaching in his pocket for his ever-present little black book.

'I can do better than that,' she replied, reaching into her bulky handbag and producing a DVD, which she handed to Knightley.

Knightley knelt by the TV set and inserted the disc into the DVD player. A silence descended over the room, including both the canines, as the disc booted up, then the TV displayed a menu. Knightley pressed 'Play' and video surveillance footage flashed up on the screen.

The image showed a night-time scene of a walled back garden – except there was a particularly strong ambient light over the proceedings.

Darkus examined the date and time code running along the top of the frame and realised. 'This was during the last full moon.'

'Indeed it was,' Fiona replied. 'Just after two o' clock in the morning as you can see . . . Here it comes now . . .'

On screen, a strange-looking beast dropped from the high wall and entered the frame. It was hairy except for the head, which hung out of sight below the shoulders in an almost Neanderthal pose. It appeared to be using the shadows to conceal itself and was walking mostly on all fours, but occasionally rearing up to stand on two. It half galloped, half crawled across the perfectly manicured lawn and followed a garden path leading around the side of the Gothic-looking property.

'I assume,' Darkus commented, 'that your perimeter wall is adjacent to the Heath?'

'Yes. Very observant,' replied Fiona.

'You'll find he's a chip off the old block – and more,' Knightley commented with his usual mix of pride and the faintest hint of professional jealousy.

The dark shape continued along the path and out of sight.

The screen flicked to another camera angle, showing an alley along the side of the house. The creature pawed hesitantly at a drainpipe, again mostly obscured by shadow, then continued towards the front of the property.

The screen flicked to a third angle as the creature leaped into frame and shambled towards the front garden and driveway. It stopped, silhouetted in the moonlight. Its head – still steeped in shadow – looked towards the surveillance camera and up at the house. Then the beast appeared to sit back on its hind legs and let out a long, tortured howl – although the footage provided no sound.

After several moments, the beast returned to all fours, raced across the driveway, quickly scaled the front gate of the property and vanished into the night.

'The hard drive stores around three weeks of footage,' explained Fiona. 'This is the only known appearance of . . . *it*. But as you can imagine, I'd like some answers.'

'Naturally,' replied Knightley.

'Have you shown this to the police, ma'am?' asked Darkus.

Fiona winced at this term of address, before answering. 'They put it down to a prank . . . But I'm not so sure. That's why I'm here.'

'Did you hear a howl that night?'

She shook her head. 'I'm an extremely deep sleeper.'

'That makes two of us,' said Knightley, before realising this information was completely irrelevant to the case.

'You know what they say. Birds of a feather . . .' said Fiona flirtatiously.

Knightley looked alarmed.

'Dad, can you replay the footage, please?'

Knightley restarted the DVD and they watched the clip again.

As the beast shambled through the front garden, then sat back and howled, Darkus signalled to his dad.

'Pause it there, if you will.'

The frame froze on the beast looking up at the house.

'Might I deduce,' Darkus began, 'that your bedroom is situated on the second floor at the front of the house?'

'Absolutely correct,' Fiona replied, somewhat surprised.

'Then I put it to you, Miss Connelly . . .' Darkus went on. 'Is it possible that this creature was somehow trying to *communicate* with you?'

'In twenty years of veterinary work, I've never encountered such a thing . . .'

'I understand this might sound odd, ma'am . . .' Darkus persisted.

'*Please* . . .' She held up a bejewelled hand. 'Call me Fifi.'

Darkus continued. 'Well, Fifi . . . From the creature's specific path and the desperation of the howl, I can only deduce that it was making a personal appeal of some kind.'

'To me?' Fiona gasped in disbelief.

Darkus nodded. 'If we were able to access footage from over three weeks ago – which sadly we can't because the hard drive will have deleted it by now – I'm willing to bet this creature visited you at the previous full moon too.'

'For what reason?' Fiona demanded. 'I train dogs, not . . .'

'Werewolves . . .' said Tilly, using the word that everyone else had been avoiding. 'Well, that is what it looks like, isn't it?'

'Young lady, there are many breeds of dog to suit many different functions and tastes. But there is *no* such thing as a werewolf. Of that I am sure,' Fiona concluded petulantly.

'What about trained attack dogs?' Darkus asked her.

'Certainly, they exist,' she replied.

'And could they, in theory, be made "smarter", and faster than they would normally be?'

'Anything is possible with a canine if the proper amount of time and effort is put in.'

'What about the use of steroids or pharmaceutical drugs?' Darkus went on. 'Such as those used in illegal dog fights.'

Fiona wrinkled her nose in disgust. 'I suppose it's possible.'

'Well, now the forum has been opened,' Knightley carried on, 'I think it's entirely possible that this beast – whatever it is – was coming to you for assistance of some kind. In fact, I believe it has been inhabiting Hampstead Heath for several months at least. And it wouldn't necessarily require a TV to know that a house full of four-legged friends is bordering its territory – or that one of the foremost dog-lovers in Britain is residing with them.'

'You're saying it's a cry for help?' said Tilly.

'Exactly that,' replied Darkus. 'But we have to work out what it is that this creature wants.'

Darkus and his dad traded a perplexed glance.

'Miss Connelly,' said Darkus, 'might I suggest we examine your property for any further clues, at your earliest convenience? Time is short. The next full moon is due tomorrow night.'

Fiona stared quizzically through her granny specs and pursed her lips. 'Of course, though you'll have to excuse the state of the house. I wasn't expecting visitors.'

'Let's say 2 p.m. then,' said Darkus. 'My father and I need to have a little chat first.'

'We do?' asked Knightley, before responding: 'Of course we do.'

'Come, Romeo.' Fiona summoned the retriever, who obediently followed her to the door, where she pulled on her clumping Hunter wellies and a raincoat. 'See you anon,' she announced and closed the door behind her.

Knightley waited a few moments before asking Darkus, 'Well, what d'you think?'

'A most peculiar development,' remarked Darkus.

'A penny for your thoughts,' his father urged.

'It's too early to say,' replied Darkus. 'The video appears to be genuine.'

'I agree,' said Tilly. 'There are no pixellation errors, the shadows and reflections look consistent.'

'But we need to go behind the pixels,' Darkus pointed out. 'It's not about what the footage shows, it's about what it *doesn't* show. A site visit may prove fruitful, even if the trail has been cold for so long it's utterly corrupted.'

Knightley harrumphed. 'If I'd known Fiona's case might be related, I would've handled it more promptly,' he complained.

'"No clue is so small that it may not be relevant to the whole",' said Darkus. 'I think you wrote that in the Knowledge once.'

'It seems my powers have been greatly diminished since then,' moaned his father.

'Then I can assume, due to your recent "episode", that

you have no memory of who attacked you on the Heath?' enquired Darkus.

'None whatsoever,' he sighed, tapping his head impatiently. 'It's locked up, up here in Fort Knox.'

Darkus nodded. 'Dad, I'm quite certain your attacker was none other than Barabas King.'

'The crime boss?' asked Knightley.

'The very same. And it appears he's behind the "smart" dog attacks across London.'

'Then what was he doing roaming the Heath?' Knightley demanded.

'I don't know. But I'm confident that between the two of us –'

'The *three* of us,' Tilly interrupted him.

Darkus continued diplomatically. 'That *between us*, a solution will present itself,' he declared. 'But first . . . I'm afraid I have a rather disturbing development of my own to impart.'

Knightley and Tilly waited patiently as Darkus fetched *The Cranston Star* newspaper from upstairs and related the surprising events that had taken place in the early hours of the morning.

Tilly stared at the inset picture of Alexis, whose blonde tresses rested on her shoulders, next to the word *Exclusive*.

'That traitor –'

'Let me see this,' interjected Knightley, scanning down the front page, reading the account of their investigation on the Heath. 'This is an unmitigated disaster,' he whispered.

Tilly wheeled on Darkus. 'Why didn't you wake me?'

Darkus shrugged defensively.

'I've got methods, you know. OK, international conventions may have been breached . . . but I get results.'

'It's already gone to press,' said Darkus. 'Which means it's already in circulation. Which means we have even less time to contain the situation before the general public get involved.'

'Well, what do you suggest?' enquired Knightley.

'We assemble the facts. Ascertain what was roaming Miss Connelly's property and how we might track it. And hope it leads to King – before the next phase of the moon.'

'We're going to need back-up,' added Tilly. 'And I have a feeling I know just the person who can help.'

Chapter 15
MEANWHILE BACK AT THE LAB

Lunch break began and the classroom emptied itself in seconds, leaving the chairs scattered and a general sense of chaos in the pupils' wake. Miss Khan couldn't tell if she'd dismissed the class or they'd dismissed her. She noted the absence of Tilly and wondered what the reason was. It could be something as mundane as a case of influenza, or something as exotic as a far-reaching criminal investigation. She had also noted the absence of Darkus – which felt too coincidental by half. The final piece of the puzzle was the dreadful accident that had confined Brendan Doyle to a locked hospital room with as yet undisclosed injuries.

Before she could let her mind wander any further, her mobile phone rang from the pocket of her lab coat. She lifted her square plastic specs and rested them on her jet-black, tied-back hair.

'Hello?' she answered the phone hesitantly.

'Miss Khan?'

'Tilly, is that you?' she asked, surprised. 'How did you get my mobile number?'

'Never mind how I got it,' replied Tilly. 'We need your assistance with something.'

'Who's we?' Miss Khan enquired, more than a little flustered. 'Has this got something to do with why you weren't in class?'

'Have you read *The Cranston Star* this morning?'

'No, I believe my copy's waiting for me in the staff-room. Along with my lunch,' she said impatiently.

'I suggest you have a look at the front page. I might as well tell you: Darkus and I are on a case.'

'Well . . .' she faltered. 'Have the police been informed?'

'They called *us*.'

'*Well* . . .' She struggled to find a suitable response. 'Has it got anything to do with what happened to poor Brendan Doyle?'

The line went silent for a moment. 'Yes,' Tilly managed. 'Yes, it has. Miss Khan, I'm going to cut to the chase. Are you able to come up with a device capable of generating a frequency that's only audible to canines?'

'You're talking about a dog whistle.'

'A high-tech version of a dog whistle, yes. Something

that could theoretically disorient, or even incapacitate, a dog. Or a wolf.'

'A *wolf*?'

'Yes or no?' insisted Tilly.

'Why, yes of course, in theory.'

'Can you come up with a functioning prototype by the next full moon?'

'That's tomorrow evening!'

'Correct.'

Miss Khan raised her eyebrows and her plastic specs inadvertently dropped back into place on the bridge of her nose. 'Well, I'll see what I can do.'

'You're a lifesaver. Quite literally. And one more thing . . .'

'Yes, Tilly?' Miss Khan wasn't used to being on the receiving end of orders, but she had to admit she found the whole thing strangely enthralling.

'Do you have any idea about the relative velocity of silver bullets?'

Miss Khan's eyes went even wider behind her specs.

Chapter 16
THE MIRROR

Crime boss Barabas King strode across the warehouse floor towards his own reflection. He'd moved between so many locations he barely remembered which warehouse it was, or where in the city he was, or where he'd been. Maybe the doctors had been right: maybe he really had detached from reality. A 'psychotic break', they had called it. He approached the shard of mirror hanging on the wall and stared deeply into it. Then he smiled wide, baring his sharpened, fang-like teeth.

Someone had once told him that if you stared at yourself in a mirror for long enough you'd be able to see all your past lives pass before your eyes. As King gazed intently into his own unusually small irises, he thought perhaps that someone had been right. Perhaps he shouldn't have killed that someone after all. They may have had more to offer on other subjects too. He ran his fingers over the rough stubble developing on his cheeks, chin and neck – thick hairs which threatened to poke through the skin and reveal the animal within.

As he continued to gape at his reflection, a long shadow appeared behind him on the wall, accompanied by a stammering male voice.

'Th-they're on to us,' the voice faltered. 'She's threatening our operation.'

King's face clouded over. 'Fiona's playing with fire . . .' he hissed. 'What d'you want me to do about it, Underwood?' he spat the villain's name out.

The long shadow drew closer, getting larger.

King snarled and continued to stare into his own eyes, until the stammering voice spoke again, more insistently.

'You work for the Combination . . . Don't f-f-fail me, King.'

Chapter 17
THE B-TEAM

Clive exited the dual carriageway, pulled up to the Little Chef restaurant and parked the Jag badly, taking up two spaces. He opened the door and several used, plastic coffee cups fell out on to the tarmac. Clive ignored them and slammed the door, further dislodging the wing mirror, which hung at an unnatural angle due to a recent collision with an old lady driving a compact car. Clive's insurance company found him liable, but Clive firmly believed the old lady must have used bribery or some other form of persuasion (cakes perhaps) in order to turn the case against him.

He cursed her as he lumbered across the car park, then momentarily forgot who he was supposed to be meeting in the first place. He racked his brain and realised yet again how impaired his 'facilities' were since that disastrous encounter with the bestselling book, *The Code*, and its evil, hypnotic mastermind, Morton

Underwood. Clive daily tried to shake off the memory of those insane events, but they still seemed to rattle around in his head like so many loose nuts and bolts.

He continued towards the entrance, passing a police Vauxhall parked subtly behind a heavy goods vehicle, and suddenly remembered the purpose of his visit.

He pushed through the heavy glass doors with the confidence of a cowboy entering his local saloon. He adjusted the trousers of his shell suit and nodded to the frail waitress at the counter. She managed a weak wave in return. Clive glanced over the booths, which were mostly empty, except for a few lorry drivers and a man in a slightly ill-fitting suit whose face was buried behind a menu at the far corner of the restaurant.

Clive ambled down the aisle, nodding to the chef, who didn't acknowledge him and carried on idly flipping burgers. As Clive arrived at the corner table, the man in the suit looked up from his menu, inspected him covertly and gestured to the seat opposite.

'Sorry I kept you waiting, Inspector,' said Clive.

'*Chief* Inspector,' replied Draycott, nervously playing with his moustache. 'And keep your voice down.'

Draycott was still smarting from his last encounter with Clive Palmer, which had left the unfortunate inspector with a broken nose and a concussion after foolishly intervening in a life-and-death struggle between Clive and his unusual stepson, Darkus, in the bathroom of Wolseley Close. Draycott never did get to the bottom of exactly what had caused Clive to have his psychotic 'benny'. Charges were never pressed, although there were chuckles and Chinese whispers at the police station about Draycott's humiliating fall from grace.

Draycott deduced that Clive's odd behaviour had something to do with the man's own fall from grace, his controversial departure from the TV programme *Wheel Spin* and his long stay in a trauma clinic, in Staffordshire apparently. And so it was with some trepidation that Draycott agreed to a surreptitious meet-up at this roadside eatery. In fact the only reason he'd even considered it was because Clive promised new information on Draycott's long-time nemesis, the dangerously strange private eye, Alan Knightley. Clive may have been an unlikely ally, but when it came to Knightley, Draycott would take his allies where he could get them. Beggars couldn't be choosers.

And besides, maybe they both had something to prove.

'What can I get you, gentlemen?' the frail waitress enquired, her hands shaking as she waited with her pen poised over her notepad.

'A cup of tea and the Works Burger,' answered Draycott precisely.

'Make that two,' added Clive. 'And the Monster Nachos please, Doreen.'

'Coming up,' she replied buoyantly, then limped off towards the kitchen.

Draycott wrinkled his moustache impatiently. 'Well, Clive? Gimme what you got.' He gestured with his hand.

Clive slid a rolled-up newspaper out of his shell suit and unfolded it on the table.

'*Cranston Star*. Breaking news. Read all about it,' Clive announced.

Draycott snatched up the paper and read the front page. He began massaging his moustache feverishly. '*Knightley* . . .' he whispered.

'And his son,' muttered Clive dismissively.

Draycott continued reading. 'A werewolf?!' he blurted. 'Hah!!'

'I have a feeling my daughter's involved too. She's been AWOL since yesterday afternoon.'

'You realise I can't involve the police without reasonable suspicion that a crime has been committed.'

'I don't want the fuzz involved.'

Draycott frowned at this crude slang for law enforcement. 'Then what *do* you want?'

'To find out what's *really* going on up there on Hampstead Heath. It's probably just a bunch of hyperactive foxes. Cute, cuddly foxes.' Clive's face went blank and he seemed to drift off for a moment.

'I believe the correct term is a *skulk* of foxes.'

'Whatever.'

'Your point being . . . ?' urged Draycott.

'I want to pool our resources, uncover the truth and discredit the Knightleys for good. A covert operation, undercover, black ops, dead of night. We catch the predator and the Knightleys are left with egg on their face. Well, what d'you say?' Clive panted. 'It'll be . . . *phe-nom-enal.*' A tiny ball of saliva formed at the corner of his mouth as he waited for Draycott's response. 'Come on, don't keep me hanging here.'

Draycott flicked through all the reasons why this would be a terrible, potentially career-ending move, before replying: 'OK, you're on.'

'Fan-tastic!' Clive erupted, before sitting down in his seat again.

So tantalising was the prospect of outwitting the 'great' Alan Knightley and his extremely odd son, that Draycott couldn't resist. 'But we do things *my* way, Clive. No showboating. This isn't TV, this is reality.'

'You took the words right out of my mouth.'

'Right. I need to think about this.'

'What sort of car will we need?' asked Clive excitedly.

'I'm thinking all-terrain. Or quad bikes. Quad bikes are awesome.'

'We need to move stealthily, under cover of night.'

'Black quad bikes.'

'No quad bikes, Clive.'

'OK.' He still looked like he had quad bikes on the brain.

'We need to get to Hampstead Heath as soon as possible, before the whole of Great Britain picks up on this story.'

Clive picked up his phone and slid it across the table. 'Might be a little late for that . . .' On the screen a national tabloid headline read: *Detectives track werewolf in London*. 'News travels fast,' said Clive.

'Then we must be faster,' replied Draycott as the food arrived. 'I'll have mine boxed up to take away.'

'Make that two, Doreen,' said Clive.

Doreen shrugged and trudged away.

At that moment, another figure entered the restaurant sporting a handlebar moustache, a combat jacket with *Burke* velcroed on it, and a pair of jogging trousers bearing the Cranston logo.

'Forgot to mention,' added Clive. 'I've enlisted some extra ground support. May I introduce Lance Corporal Burke from Cranston's PE department.'

Burke nudged in beside him. 'Unavoidable delay. Man down on the rugger pitch.'

207

Clive patted him on the shoulder. 'Burke's encountered the Knightleys before – Darkus, to be exact, during one of my daughter's escape attempts. He also has a background in army special operations.'

'Really?' said Draycott dubiously.

'Territorials. The Rock,' replied Burke.

'Alcatraz?' asked Draycott, confused.

'Gibraltar,' the teacher corrected him.

'Ah,' said Draycott, looking him over. 'Nice facial hair.'

'Ditto,' said Burke.

'Trust me,' Clive went on. 'Ray is a good man in a fight. And he's got some sweet gadgets. So are we ready to rock 'n' roll or what?'

Clive raised his hand to Draycott in a high five.

Draycott winced but couldn't disguise the eager smile spreading under his moustache. He extended his hand and smacked it triumphantly against Clive's.

'But no funny business,' Draycott warned him, pointing at his newfound ally with the long finger of the law.

'Cub's honour,' replied Clive, giving the three-finger salute, but knowing full well he'd earned a lifetime ban for tying another scout's tent to the trailer hitch of a four-by-four. 'It's *showtime*!'

Chapter 18
DUSTING FOR
PAW PRINTS

At just before 2 p.m. Knightley drove the Fairway cab along East Heath Road, past the park in question, with Darkus and Tilly observing it from the back windows. A persistent rain was sheeting down over the trees and meadows, making the leaves shimmer with a sinister quality, and leaving a scattering of pock marks on the surface of the ponds. A few determined dog walkers were the only signs of life on the Heath; their heads down, braced against the weather.

As they passed the car park, Darkus spotted a small mobile broadcast van with a radar dish, a cameraman setting up his gear and a female reporter clutching her notes – an older version of Alexis, he thought to himself. The same wave of blonde hair, the tailored outfit, the long legs. The news channel's logo was plastered across the side of the van.

Tilly almost seemed to read his mind. 'Tabloid vultures . . .' she muttered.

Inexplicably, Tilly had changed her own hair to blonde in the short space of time between Fiona Connelly leaving and their departure to examine her residence. Darkus didn't know if this was inspired by Alexis's picture in the paper or not, but it was a traditional, Hollywood glamour look for Tilly and Darkus thought it suited her well.

'What are you looking at?' she challenged him.

'Your hair. It looks very . . . blonde,' said Darkus.

'I need to keep changing it to avoid unwanted attention, that's all. There's nothing more to it than that.'

'I just thought it looked nice,' answered Darkus, baffled.

'Your comment has been noted.' Tilly pulled on a knit cap and looked out of the window.

Also, quite inexplicably, Uncle Bill had insisted on meeting them at the Connelly residence, although it was difficult to guess what he would bring to the party. His powers of detection were limited, his powers of reasoning even more so; and his white Transit van (or mobile command centre, or 'Moby Dick' as he commonly referred to it) was only useful for live tracking in real time – and Fiona Connelly's back garden was most definitely a 'cold scene'.

Bill had, however, provided them with an update on Barabas King. Someone matching King's description was seen leaving a South London warehouse earlier that day in the company of several hoodies and a pack of Rottweilers. The gang were seen entering a convoy of blacked-out minicabs, but the vehicles were soon lost in London traffic, which abounds with blacked-out minicabs.

It was clear that King was an expert at remaining off the radar. With the clock ticking until the full moon, Darkus was left with an intriguing array of clues, but no line of reasoning to link them all together. The 'smart' dogs were acting on King's orders and picking off senior police officers from SO 42. But who was pulling King's strings? How did Fiona's intruder fit in? And who or what was responsible for the atrocities on the Heath?

As the Knightleys' Fairway cab pulled up at the gated driveway, they found Uncle Bill already waiting on the street outside, shifting on his feet. Before a word could be exchanged, the electric gates whirred open, welcoming the team to the Connelly residence.

Knightley parked next to Fiona's champagne-coloured Volvo estate while Uncle Bill jogged up the driveway after them, finding himself nearly pinched by the swiftly closing gates.

'Glad you could make it,' said Knightley.

'Would nae miss this for the world, Alan,' Bill puffed. 'Fiona Connelly is a national treasure.' He lowered his voice privately. 'And a nice plate of rumbledethumps.'

'Come again?' asked Knightley, having no idea what Bill meant.

'Spot o' eeksy-peeksy,' said Bill.

'Again?' repeated Knightley.

'Braw wifie.'

'Once more.'

'She's an extremely attractive lady, Alan,' he exclaimed.

'But I thought you . . . and Bogna . . . ?' Knightley trailed off.

'A man should never tie himself doon, Alan. Nae at my age,' said Bill, although it wasn't clear if he meant he was too old, or too young.

Darkus, Tilly and Wilbur got out of the cab and surveyed the Victorian Gothic façade of the house. At that moment the front door opened and a dozen golden retrievers, Labradors, collies and terriers flooded out on to the gravel path.

'Lovers! Wait!' Fiona appeared at the door, a vision in a long flowy skirt and a heaving blouse.

The dogs leaped about merrily, jumping up on the guests and cavorting in the driveway. Wilbur stood his ground apprehensively, keeping a safe distance, raising his snout to avoid the sniffs, licks and general smothering, until a sharp command stopped the dogs in their tracks.

'Sit!!'

Knightley and Uncle Bill snapped to attention. The dogs froze and sat down on the spot. All eyes turned to Fiona as her commanding scowl unwound into a gentle smile and she lightly clapped her hands together.

'Good boys and girls. Now let's give our guests a warm, *calm*, canine welcome.' The dogs trotted inside obediently on either side of Fiona's thick legs whose cankles protruded from the bottom of her skirt, encased in compression stockings and Birkenstock sandals. 'All of you. Do come in.' Wilbur sniffed around her feet and wagged his tail by way of a greeting. 'Yes, that includes you.' She petted him fondly.

Uncle Bill doffed his hat and led the way. 'Ah'm from Scotland Yard, madam,' he began. 'The name's Billoch. Montague Billoch. Most people call me Bill.'

'Well, hel-lo, Bill,' Fiona warbled. 'It is reassuring to have a genuine officer of the law in the house.'

'Aye. Ye can call me Monty, if ye like.'

'And *ye*,' she playfully imitated him, 'may call me Fifi. Now how about a cup of tea and some chocolate Hobnobs?'

Bill turned to Knightley with his mouth hanging ajar. 'Ye see, Alan,' he whispered excitedly. '*Marriage material*.'

Knightley shrugged and headed inside.

'Dad?' Darkus spoke up. 'Tilly and I are going stay out here and examine the perimeter.'

Fiona turned to address them, linking her arm in Bill's. 'I've turned the security system off, so you can work unhindered.'

'Good plan,' Knightley answered and awkwardly followed the fledgling lovebirds into the house.

Darkus and Tilly looked at each other and silently got to work, heading in the direction of the back garden. Darkus studied the gravel but found it had been thoroughly turned over by paw and foot traffic and ploughed by parking cars. They crossed over a short paved patio and proceeded round the side of the house, arriving at a tall security gate, which had deliberately been left open for them.

Darkus examined a steel locking mechanism located halfway up the gate with a small pad on either side of it.

Tilly put her finger on the pad and a red light illuminated it, followed by a sharp error tone. 'Biometric scanner on both sides,' she explained. 'Reads fingerprints. Only approved guests allowed.'

Darkus nodded, inspecting the high gate and the black metal railings on either side. 'I suppose it must have scaled it then,' he said, raising himself on tiptoes and looking as high as he could.

Tilly left him there and continued into the back garden. Darkus caught up with her, grabbing her arm before she stepped on the grass.

'Wait,' he cautioned.

The lawn was scattered with several different sizes of dog faeces. Darkus stooped down and surveyed the turf, looking for any bent blades of grass. But it had been well trodden by dogs, gardeners and foxes. There were no obvious tracks.

'It's a minefield,' commented Tilly, stepping over the small brown mounds and approaching the high brick wall that encircled the garden.

Beyond the wall were the dense trees and overgrown foliage of Hampstead Heath, barely tamed beyond the property line. For someone as security conscious as Fiona Connelly, it must have been daunting to have this barren wilderness merely metres from where she slept – with all its nocturnal inhabitants very much awake.

Darkus followed Tilly, picking his way across the grass and examining the brickwork. He then noted a length of black plastic tubing running along the edge of the wall and vanishing under the turf of the lawn.

'Plastic conduit for running wiring,' Tilly went on. She spotted several more lengths of conduit protruding from the edge of the lawn in various places. 'My guess is it's buried fibre-optic cable. Detects intruders within seconds and relays a message back to the security hub. High-end stuff. If you know how to use it.'

'Interesting,' commented Darkus and continued his survey of the back garden, stopping on a section of flower bed.

'What is it?' said Tilly.

Darkus knelt down and angled his phone on an odd arrangement of shapes in the earth. 'Looks like a partial paw print.'

'If that's a partial . . . the paw must have been –'

'Massive. Precisely,' said Darkus, photographing the print from several angles.

Moments later, they walked back round to the gravel driveway and entered the front door.

Fiona was already holding court in the sitting room, pouring tea into china cups for Knightley and Bill.

'I'll be mother . . .' she whispered.

The dozen or so dogs were sitting and lying in various states of repose around the room, which was decorated with a heavily floral motif. Wilbur sat at ease in the corner, silently examining the others.

'The theory behind my long-running TV series,' Fiona went on, 'is that there is *no* such thing as a *bad* dog.' She set down the teapot and plopped down into an armchair. 'Dogs, like humans, can be educated and encouraged to be valuable members of society. Every one of God's creatures has the ability to redeem itself. My job is to give our four-legged friends the

216

practical tools with which to harness their more barbaric tendencies and help them live under human rule.'

Bill nodded eagerly, reaching for the Hobnobs with a pair of sugar tongs.

Fiona added milk to her tea and continued: 'After all, dogs began as wolves, before they were brought to heel. They descend from the same DNA. Dogs are merely wolves that have been bred to love instead of attack. Just like we humans are descended from the barbaric cavemen – and yet now we sit here, having a nice, civilised cup of tea.'

Darkus noticed that a thin layer of dog hair still clung to the carpets and furniture. An elderly housekeeper worked urgently on a chaise longue with a large lint roller that was rapidly resembling a furry paw. She tore off the hairy bit and kept rolling.

Fiona looked up at Darkus and Tilly as they approached the sofa. 'Did you find anything of interest?'

'Nothing yet,' Tilly lied.

Knightley looked puzzled. Bill shrugged and dunked another biscuit into his teacup, munching happily.

'It would be useful, with your permission, Fifi,' Darkus carried on, 'if we could examine the rest of the house for possible points of ingress.'

'He means places where the beast might have attempted entry,' Bill clarified in between mouthfuls.

'I see. Of course,' said Fiona and gestured with a bejewelled hand. 'Be my guest.'

Darkus nodded to Tilly and they left the tea party to begin their search of the inside.

They moved through the high-ceilinged reception rooms, kitchen and utility rooms on the ground floor, each detective focusing in on their particular area of expertise. Darkus examined the floors, furnishings and windows, while Tilly studied the shelves, ceilings and security features.

A door under the stairs opened on to a narrow set of steps leading down to the basement. It had been converted into a private gym complete with sound-proofed walls and two matching treadmills – presumably one was for the 'life partner' Fiona was obviously on the hunt for. The windows were locked and reinforced with shatterproof glass and Darkus had to admit the house was very secure.

They worked their way upwards, sweeping the building efficiently, ducking into cloakrooms and toilets, before ascending a grand staircase to the upper floors. A series of bedrooms were all decorated in shabby chic and each contained a cluster of baskets, torn pillows and dog bowls. Clearly, these animals really *were* Fiona's family and they had the run of the house. The stench of canine scent was musky and overpowering. Tilly pulled her sweatshirt over her nose and led the way to the master bedroom.

Fiona's bedchamber boasted a grand four-poster bed which was also surrounded by dog baskets. Her bedspread was covered in a thin layer of matted hair.

Darkus approached the bed cautiously, then took a pair of latex gloves from his top pocket and snapped them on.

'What are you doing?' Tilly whispered.

'Just checking for bedfellows . . .'

Darkus gently lifted the hairy bedspread, then the rest of the bedclothes fell away to reveal two heavy indentations, pressed into the soft mattress topper. One shape was human and had a gigantic woman's nightie discarded by it. The other shape appeared to be a large, curled-up animal of some kind and was accompanied by a large thatch of bristly hair.

'What *is* that?' Tilly murmured, wrinkling her nose.

'The hair of a large dog, it would appear.'

Tilly cocked her head. 'Wait a second. You're not suggesting that thing out there . . . might have been . . . up here?'

'I'm not suggesting anything,' said Darkus. 'I'm merely postulating ideas until I find one that supports all the facts.'

Darkus took out his phone and aimed it at the mattress, flash-photographing the evidence; then

219

carefully replaced the bedclothes and bedspread, removed the gloves and put them in their own Ziploc bag, before tucking them in his pocket.

Tilly examined the panic button located on Fiona's side of the bed, which would alert the police in the event of an intruder. Darkus continued into the ensuite bathroom and examined the bathtub and shower cubicle. Another thick knot of hair blocked the plughole of the tub. Darkus plucked it out with a pair of tweezers, then deposited the evidence in another Ziploc and stashed it. Next he surveyed the tiled floor, noting some partial footprints between the shower and the bath. He knelt down and photographed them, before pocketing the phone and exiting the room.

Darkus re-entered the sitting room with Tilly in tow. Fiona, Knightley and Bill looked up expectantly.

'I can see no evidence of a break-in,' announced Darkus.

'Well, that's reassuring,' sighed Fiona, relieved.

Knightley got to his feet. 'Do you need us to have a second look?'

Bill stood up gamely, wiping crumbs from his chin.

Darkus looked to Tilly who shook her head.

'It's not necessary,' replied Darkus. 'We've seen everything we need to see.'

*

The whole party emerged from the front door, flanked by retrievers, collies and terriers, who all seemed disappointed to be saying goodbye.

'So, what's the verdict?' Knightley muttered to his son under his breath.

'It's too early to say,' Darkus replied in hushed tones.

'I wish you'd stop saying that,' his father snipped.

'You used to say the same thing.'

'You could've at least given me a chance to look around. Even if my powers of reasoning are in a poor state of repair compared to yours.'

'I take no pleasure in that fact, Dad.'

'Then you agree – they *are*.'

'Dad, I don't think us arguing about your ability to reason soundly is going to help us solve this case.'

'You're so irritatingly logical.'

'You were once too. So logical you didn't bother with the less logical things in life . . . like me and Mum.'

'Let's not dredge up past history. We've got a case on the boil.'

'Agreed. And I did find one "smoking gun" in the back garden . . . although I'm not sure if it fires silver bullets.' Darkus showed his father the picture of the partial paw print on his phone.

'It's a match for the one on the Heath!' said Knightley.

'Let's not tell the whole world,' warned Darkus.

They were interrupted by Fiona calling out from the boot room.

'It's a shame you can't stay . . .' she commiserated. 'It's nearly time for walkies. Our favourite time of the day.' The dogs started leaping in muted excitement.

'Well, as it happens,' Bill interjected, 'my doctor has instructed me tae take regular exercise for my leg. Ten thousand steps a day in fact.' He rummaged deep in his coat pockets and pulled out a digital pedometer. 'And it so happens I have the rest ay the day aff.'

Knightley and Darkus looked at each other in disbelief.

Fiona's eyes appeared to flinch before she responded, 'Then you must join us, Monty. Mustn't he, lovers?' The dogs jumped for joy, on the point of barking, but restraining themselves.

Fiona reached for a long coat rack, draped almost entirely with dog leads.

Bill turned to Knightley. 'Alan, ah'm going to handle this investigation *personally*. Ah'll report back later . . . or tomorrow mornin'.' He winked and raised his thick eyebrows all in one motion.

Knightley frowned. 'I'll wait for your call.'

Darkus and his father returned to the Fairway with Tilly and Wilbur, then the cab performed a tight U-turn and exited through the opening driveway gates. Fiona activated the house alarm and strolled on to the street, arm in arm with Bill, encircled by canines great and small. The gates closed automatically behind them.

Darkus watched the odd couple with concern from the back seat. 'Do you think his judgement has been impaired?'

'Thoroughly,' answered Knightley. 'You remember what I told you about females, Doc . . .'

'Yes, but I'm not sure you actually believe it. You said they're a distraction,' said Darkus with a hint of resentment.

Tilly piped up from the glass divider behind Knightley's head. 'Ah-ah! You're not getting rid of me that easily. Not this time. A bit of feminine intuition never hurt anyone.' She examined the scene. 'Fiona's clearly not interested in him.'

'And he's following her around like a puppy,' added Darkus, watching Bill gallantly squire Fiona and her procession of dogs along the pavement in the direction of the Heath.

'I fear we have yet another problem to add to our list,' complained Knightley.

Chapter 19
A VISIT FROM THE QUARTERMASTER

As they arrived at 27 Cherwell Place, Darkus spotted two further issues. The first was a scruffily dressed male reporter with a long-lensed camera loitering at the street corner. The second was a pair of Rottweilers casually sniffing around some rubbish bins at the top of the road, as if they'd been instructed to 'act natural'. The reporter began bombarding the black cab with flash photographs as it pulled up outside the address.

The Knightleys and Tilly hopped out, their heads hung low, and hurried to the door, which Bogna was already holding open for them. Wilbur stood guard on the pavement, staring down the Rottweilers who were watching from their vantage point in silence.

The reporter followed his targets to the property line, snapping frame after frame.

The Rottweilers witnessed the melee from a safe distance and decided not to act.

'Alan?' the reporter shouted. 'What do you say to the rumours of a werewolf on Hampstead Heath?'

Knightley squinted in the glare of the flashbulb. 'No comment.'

'Darkus? What about you?' he persisted.

'Same as my father I'm afraid. No comment.'

'What about *you*?' The reporter turned to Tilly.

'Why don't you hack my phone and find out?' she began. 'Hold on, I've got a better idea: I'll hack *yours*, find out where you live, find out what you're hiding, tell your wife and family. Upload it all over the web. How'd you like that?'

The reporter lowered his camera, looking dumb-founded. Tilly vanished inside after the Knightleys and the door slammed in his face.

Inside, Bogna hung their coats for them and directed them to the living room where she explained they had a guest waiting.

Miss Khan sat politely poised on the edge of the sofa, with a stainless steel briefcase at her feet and a plate of Bogna's sandwiches uneaten before her. She stood up as Tilly introduced her.

'Alan, this is Miss Khan from school. She's the extra assistance I told you about.'

'Glad to meet you,' said Knightley, extending his hand formally.

'I've heard a great deal about you, Mr Knightley.'

'All good I hope –'

'But I've not seen you at any parents' days,' she continued.

'I was having a . . . somewhat extended sabbatical.'

'I understand you woke up last October. There was an open day just before Christmas.'

Knightley's brow shifted, looking scolded. 'You're right, I will make more of an effort next time.' He straightened his tie awkwardly, appearing somewhat taken with this rather unyielding character. 'You have my undivided attention.'

'To business . . .' she went on.

She opened the stainless steel briefcase to reveal a foam cut-out containing three small cylindrical devices.

'I brought some extra double-A batteries with me, in case you don't have any.' She plucked the devices out and handed one each to Darkus, Tilly and Knightley. 'When you press this button, it emits a high-pitched ultrasonic frequency which will intimidate and disturb any dog . . . or wolf . . . within a hundred-metre radius. In fact it might even disturb very young children, because their powers of hearing are far more advanced than ours. But hopefully there won't be any young babies in the vicinity.'

'I certainly hope not,' Knightley assured her.

'To switch it off, simply press it again. It could make the difference between getting away, or not. Depending of course on what you're seeking to get away from.'

'We're not at liberty to say at this point, Miss Khan,' said Darkus. 'Partly for confidentiality reasons and partly because we're not entirely sure *what* it is we're dealing with.'

'I've read *The Cranston Star*. I know what they're speculating.'

'I prefer to deal in facts,' answered Darkus.

'Where do you stand on the supernatural, Miss Khan?' Knightley pressed her.

'My family believed in myths and legends,' she replied. 'My father had certain gods he prayed to. I, however, prefer the answers that science provides us with. I find them more reliable.'

'And what if you were confronted by something you couldn't explain scientifically?' Knightley insisted.

'Then, Mr Knightley, I will let you know if and when that happens.'

'Perhaps one day you will and then we can discuss this further.'

Knightley seemed to relish the prospect of a future exchange. He betrayed the vaguest glint in his eye, like an unpolished diamond buried deep in the rough of his often brusque demeanour. Darkus suddenly realised that his father dearly wanted someone to unearth that gem – whether it was Jackie, or another person who might be better equipped to know what sort of care it required. That person was the missing piece of the puzzle that had kept his father searching and investigating all this time, as a means to fill the void. Darkus feared his dad would never be truly happy until someone appreciated what he'd kept hidden inside all these years.

'Until then,' replied Miss Khan, 'you'll find me at the next parents' day . . . along with all Darkus's other teachers, who I'm sure would be very curious to meet you too. For the record, he, and Tilly here, are top-notch students. Top of the class.'

'I have no doubt.' Knightley beamed with pride.

'Though their attendance record leaves a lot to be desired.' Miss Khan turned to Darkus and Tilly. 'Speaking of which, I must return to Cranston before my absence triggers any alarm bells. I trust I'll see you both back at school safely . . . By the end of the week, please, Mr Knightley.'

'Wait . . . How's Brendan?' Tilly asked the teacher.

'I don't know. It's immediate family only at the hospital. The first task was identifying him. It'll be a slow, painful recovery.'

Tilly went pale, then swallowed. 'Please keep me posted,' she insisted.

'Of course,' replied Miss Khan.

Darkus nodded awkwardly, unsure how to feel about Brendan Doyle. The bully had made Darkus's life hell, but no one deserved what the boy would have to endure. Doyle's fate had been dealt so quickly and violently that it almost scared Darkus more than any other facet of the case.

'Perhaps I can see you out, Miss Khan,' said Knightley. 'With all the press attention, I think it's better we're not photographed together.'

'Very wise.'

Miss Khan pulled a headscarf over her jet-black hair and moved to the entrance hall. Bogna placed her hands together in her version of a Hindu farewell and ushered her out of the front door.

Darkus climbed the stairs to his father's office to get a bird's-eye view of the street. Fortunately the reporter had gone, possibly heeding Tilly's warning, or perhaps having got all the photographs he required. Darkus watched from the window as Miss Khan walked briskly to the top of the road, approaching the two Rottweilers who were still loitering with intent.

Suddenly anxious that Miss Khan may have become a target by association, Darkus reached through the open office window and held out the ultrasonic device she'd given him. He pressed the button.

The two Rottweilers reacted immediately, shaking their heads with irritation, as if trying to rid themselves of an unseen insect. Miss Khan passed them without incident and turned on to the main road, vanishing from sight. Satisfied that the gadget would prove useful, Darkus switched it off and closed the window.

The dogs shook off their discomfort and trotted away in the opposite direction, leaving Cherwell Place deserted.

Darkus turned to the doorway and found Wilbur whimpering on the landing, his ears flat against his head. Darkus looked down at the ultrasonic dog whistle and realised it would have been equally painful for him.

'Oh no – sorry, boy, I didn't think.' Wilbur came to heel and Darkus ruffled the dog's fur.

He looked around his father's office, noting the rows of reference books, the solitary office chair and the mahogany desk, accented with Carpathian elm. Darkus wondered to himself whether this was what the future had in store for him as well – like father, like son. It was a lonely existence, one devoted to details, formulas and technicalities. Some might even call it a devotion to the trivial, until of course these elements were arranged into a logical pattern in order to solve the crime. But surely when a mind was so focused on the details, it might miss the wood for the trees. Maybe the really important things in life could not be examined, catalogued and explained. Maybe they were what took place between the clues and behind the scenes, while detectives were too busy detecting things.

'What's on your mind?' Tilly interrupted him from the doorway.

'Tonight is the last night before the full moon,' Darkus replied. 'We can only hope the press coverage peaks before King lets the dogs out.'

'I'm more worried about the Heath,' she replied. 'By tomorrow night, that place is going to be crawling with looky-loos and have-a-go heroes. I only hope they don't run into whatever's creeping around up there –'

'Wait . . .' Darkus interrupted her and moved towards the sofa urgently.

'What's wrong?'

Hung over the edge of the sofa was his father's tweed jacket – except for a small square of fabric that had been cut away from the arm. A piece of frayed silk lining was poking out in its place. The catastrophiser started humming and rattling.

'Dad – ?' Darkus called out.

A thundering on the stairs heralded Bogna's arrival with an ever-present tray of sandwiches. 'Something is wrong? I was just preparing sandwich.'

His father appeared behind her. 'What is it, Doc?'

'Was there some kind of accident with your jacket?' Darkus demanded.

'Not that I know of,' said Knightley.

Bogna approached the offending hole in the garment. 'Who has done this to Alan's nice jacket?' she asked, outraged.

Darkus looked to Wilbur but the dog didn't exhibit any of his traditional guilty signs – and besides, he was a reformed character. 'It wasn't Wilbur,' he confirmed.

Bogna tried unsuccessfully to press the lining back into the hole. 'Who would do such a thing?'

'The Combination,' Knightley answered. 'I fear they're behind this. And I can only deduce that I have now been targeted *personally*.'

Tilly nodded. 'Every dog-attack victim lost an article of clothing in the run-up to the full moon.'

'It's how they track you,' agreed Darkus grimly, nodding to the office window. 'The lock's been forced. Someone must have got in while we were talking to Miss Khan.'

'Now let's not get hysterical,' Knightley assured them. 'It'll take more than a few trained mutts to take down Alan Knightley.'

Bogna, Darkus and Tilly looked at each other, appearing less convinced.

'Especially now that we have Miss Khan's high-tech dog whistles,' Knightley went on.

'I don't fancy their chances against a werewolf,' Tilly suggested.

'Hopefully none of us will get close enough to find out,' said Darkus.

'So you concede a supernatural presence is at work?' his father asked him.

'I concede nothing. I discount nothing,' Darkus responded. 'We have members of SO 42 marked for death at the jaws of King's attack dogs. And we have a particularly fierce creature picking off victims at random on Hampstead Heath and visiting a well-known TV personality. All during the full moon. What connects these bizarre events is something I'm still working on.'

'Well, now's no time to hold anything back,' said Knightley, sounding more coherent and more fearful than usual. 'Share your theories.'

'OK,' agreed Darkus. 'But first, what do we know about Fiona Connelly? Tilly . . . ?'

Tilly tapped on her phone and typed in a search. Within moments she was reading a short bio of Fiona Connelly.

'Fiona was raised and educated in Kenya, East Africa. An only child, born of white parents of British descent who reportedly ran a wildlife park near Mombasa before dying in a safari accident, leaving Fiona an orphan. Fiona assembled a host of veterinary qualifications in

233

Kenya before making the move to Britain five years ago, arriving as a relative unknown. She quickly impressed the "powers that be" in the TV world with her knowledge and understanding of dog behaviour and, well, the rest is history. She's written two bestselling dog behaviour guides and has been a judge at Crufts. She is unmarried and has not been linked to any significant others, in the public eye, or otherwise.'

'Thanks, Tilly,' said Darkus. 'Now I'll tell you what *I* know – or rather what I can *prove*,' he announced, pausing for effect. 'Whatever was in Fiona's garden was permitted entry into it.'

'What?' exclaimed Knightley.

'How?' enquired Tilly.

'We saw footage of the creature moving along the side of the house to the front of the property,' explained Darkus. 'But, as you observed yourself, Tilly, the fingerprint scanner on the side gate has sensors on both sides – therefore, the creature could not have passed in or out of that door unless it was an approved person, with fingerprints.'

'Surely it could've just scaled the fence?' argued Knightley.

'I discounted that possibility for the simple reason that there were no scratch or scuff marks on the black metal railings. I checked carefully. Nothing has scaled that fence,' Darkus stated with conviction. 'As I said before, it's not about what the footage shows, but what it doesn't show. We never saw the creature cross that threshold. It's as if whoever let the creature on to the property wanted to disguise the fact that they had done so.'

'Are you saying Fiona deliberately let that thing on to her own property?' Tilly asked.

'Either she did, or someone with access to her security system did,' replied Darkus. 'Security is tight. So tight that someone *had* to have known about the intruder.'

'A-plus,' said Knightley. 'I take my hat off to you, Doc.'

'I still don't have a complete solution to the facts,' Darkus complained. 'If you'd allow me a few hours alone with my thoughts, I may be able to find one.'

Knightley raised his eyebrows, realising he was being ejected from his own office. 'OK, I'll make a cup of tea and see if I can raise Uncle Bill.'

'Tilly, perhaps you could look at whether we can bypass Fiona's security system for our own purposes. I suspect we'll need to conduct further surveillance on the property tomorrow.'

'I'm on it,' she replied.

'Dinner is served at seven thirty,' Bogna added. 'It will be a collection of cold meats and cheeses, including hard-boiled eggs, delicious blood sausage and favourite kielbasa sticks.'

'Yum,' said Knightley, then retreated to the door, leaving Darkus alone at the desk.

'Wilbur,' said Darkus, 'you can stay.'

The German shepherd wagged his tail and sat obediently by his master.

Chapter 20
AMATEUR NIGHT

The sun sank below the trees surrounding Hampstead Heath and the handful of street lamps at the East Heath Road entrance flickered to life.

A light mist began to creep in over the meadows as a cameraman packed the last of his equipment into a mobile broadcast van. His blonde reporter companion hopped into the passenger seat, the doors slammed shut and the van pulled out of the now empty car park.

A few moments later, an unmarked police Vauxhall drove in and parked in a far corner, switching off its lights. A few moments after that, a customised open-top Land Rover with a steel roll cage and a vertical exhaust accelerated into the car park and skidded to a halt in a cloud of dust.

Chief Inspector Draycott grimaced and stepped gingerly out of his Vauxhall in a black polo neck and permanent crease trousers. He wafted away the dust to find Clive Palmer grinning at the wheel of the Land Rover, with Lance Corporal Burke standing behind him on a makeshift weapons platform, wearing full camouflage and a pair of night-vision goggles.

'Tell me you don't actually have a machine gun on that thing?' Draycott demanded.

'Of course not,' replied Clive, leaning out of the window. 'But Ray's brought his crossbow. Just in case.'

Burke held the weapon aloft in a silent battle cry.

'No four-by-fours,' commanded Draycott. 'No crossbows.'

'I knew you were going to say that.' Clive jumped down from the vehicle to reveal he was wearing an all black shell suit and matching trainers. He walked around to the back and released the tailgate. 'Which is why I brought these . . .'

Clive took out three BMX bicycles and lined them up against the car.

'Aren't we a little old for this sort of thing?' asked Draycott, before finding himself strangely taken with the bikes.

'These are from my personal collection. I'm taking that one . . .' Clive pointed to his favourite, which had black plastic wheels. 'You can argue it out over the other two.' Then he added privately to Draycott,

'But I wouldn't upset Ray. He's got a *very* short fuse.'

Burke leaped down from the back of the Land Rover and shouldered a military backpack. Draycott gave the man some distance, before turning to Clive, who was hoisting a large, heavy sports bag on to his back.

Draycott recoiled, turning up his nose. 'What in God's name is that *smell*?'

'Lion dung,' said Clive with a wink. 'Stole it from Chessington World of Adventures.'

'Why would you do that?!' Draycott implored.

'It's a well-known deterrent to foxes and other predators,' Clive explained. 'Makes 'em think there's a "big cat" around. Scares the pants off 'em.'

'Not as stupid as he looks,' commented Burke.

'Thank you, Ray,' Clive added.

'OK,' admitted Draycott. 'This is not as bad as I was expecting. Let's saddle up and do some good.'

'Amen, brother,' replied Clive.

On the other side of the Heath, at the entrance to Parliament Hill Fields, a female figure walked intrepidly in a thick anorak and woolly hat, holding a flashlight. Slightly embarrassingly, she also held a crucifix, although it was buried deep in her jacket pocket out of sight, clutched in a gloved hand. Alexis didn't believe in all that supernatural stuff, but she still decided to err on the side of caution.

'Come on, Ian!' she called behind her.

A lanky adolescent figure, Ian Dulwich, ambled to keep up with her. 'Coming . . .' he said gallantly, although he was weighed down by a long-lensed camera and a fully laden rucksack with several water flasks swinging from it.

She turned to chastise him. 'It's not enough to just break the story – I've already got every major news outlet chomping at the bit. Now it's about the follow-up . . . the *wow* moment . . . the National Geographic shot. If we, or rather *you*, can get a snap of this thing, whatever it turns out to be, then we're talking worldwide acclaim. I'm talking the Loch Ness monster, Big Foot. Proper myth and legend stuff.'

'Whatever you say, Lex.' Ian shifted the rucksack and attempted to stretch out his back.

'According to the witness report the epicentre of the activity is Parliament Hill.' She pointed up the steep, dark incline towards the summit, just visible on the skyline.

'It looks like an awfully long way up . . .' Ian pointed out. 'And it doesn't look like anyone else is around. I mean . . . no one could hear us scream.'

'I'm not intending to scream, Ian. Are you?' Alexis challenged him.

'Of course not,' he backtracked. 'I'm just saying . . .'

'Last one up's a sissy,' she ordered and took off up the hill, with one hand swinging confidently, while the other one still clutched the crucifix, out of sight.

On the opposite side of Parliament Hill, the sound of three panting cyclists could be heard over the background hum of the city and the occasional birdcall from the wilderness. Clive Palmer, Chief Inspector Draycott and Lance Corporal Burke hyperventilated as they leaned down on the pedals with all their middle-aged spread, coaxing their undersized BMXs up the arduous hill from the ponds. The path was overarched with tall, ancient trees and thick foliage on all sides. The bikes had no lights but could just be seen in the dim light of the not yet full moon.

'I . . . can't . . . go . . . one . . . centimetre . . . further.' Clive stopped pedalling and almost began to roll backwards down the hill until he painfully dismounted. 'My L-5 vertebra is bloody killing me.'

'Maybe it's that sack of steaming lion excrement on your back,' snapped Draycott. 'I mean, if there is something out there, it's going to smell us a mile off. And you did insist on these stupid bikes,' he complained. 'I've got a perfectly good mountain bike at home. With pannier bags and everything.'

'If you two are finished comparing your tackle, can we take this hill?' Burke advised, before surveying the scene. 'Switching to infrared.' He pulled down his night-vision goggles, tapped his head and said, 'Follow my lead.' He then pumped his fist in the air and continued pedalling heavily uphill.

Draycott groaned and continued after him. 'If my wife knew I was riding without a helmet, there'd be hell to pay.'

Clive rubbed his lower back and kept walking, pushing the bike beside him. Suddenly, the heavens opened up and started pouring with rain.

'Fan-bloody-tastic –'

Then a noise stopped him. A high-pitched crying noise, almost like a baby.

'Guys?' Clive called after the others who were almost out of sight at the upper edge of the woods. 'Oh, guuuuys . . . ?' Clive started walking faster, pushing the BMX uphill more urgently. 'Wait for me!'

Burke and Draycott leaned against their bikes at the top of the tree-lined path. Behind them, the grassy banks of Parliament Hill stretched up to the grey, foreboding sky.

Clive arrived in a hurry, his bike toppling to the ground as he clutched his chest. 'I heard something. Like a baby crying –' he gasped.

'Probably foxes,' said Burke. 'It's rutting season.'

'Perfect,' announced Draycott. 'Then it's all the work of some randy foxes and the Knightleys think they're chasing a werewolf? Those *amateurs*! Just wait until we solve this case, hand it over to Bill Oddie or Bear Grylls and have our moment in the limelight.'

Suddenly a much louder noise echoed through the trees around them. It was a tortured howl – like the distress horn of a sinking ocean liner.

'That didn't sound like a fox,' whispered Clive.

'No. It didn't,' agreed Draycott.

Burke scanned the undergrowth with his night-vision goggles. A large shape appeared to move through the trees on his infrared. 'Stay calm, people. The hostile seems to be a quarter of a klick due north of our position. When engaging the enemy it's vital to maintain the element of surprise –'

Burke was interrupted by another fearsome howl, which lasted longer and reached an even more terrifying pitch.

'Surprise?' hissed Draycott. 'You really think it hasn't already smelled us? Or rather *him*.' He jabbed a finger at Clive.

Clive checked his watch. 'Oh, bum. I promised Jackie I'd be home for *MasterChef*,' he improvised. 'I'd better get going –'

'Ah-ah, not so fast,' said Draycott. 'You got us into this mess in the first place. I want to know what's going on up here. Deserters will be court-martialled.'

'I second that,' added Burke.

'Bl-oody hell, all-right . . .' Clive moaned.

'Platoon, move out!' Burke ordered.

The troop pushed their bicycles in the direction of the sound, along the path at the base of Parliament Hill.

Meanwhile, Alexis and Ian tramped across the other side of the hill, with a distant spire behind them, which was just a vague shadow on the skyline. They crossed the apex and descended through a small wooded outcrop, arriving at a fallen tree stretched dramatically across the meadow before them.

Then they froze, also hearing the howl echoing through the woods.

'Er . . . Lex?' Ian piped up, his water bottles rattling. 'Did you hear that?'

'Sure did. And it sounded like it was coming from behind those trees.'

She pointed to a small, dark gap in the undergrowth.

'Er, don't you think,' suggested Ian, 'perhaps, we should call for help?'

'What, and let someone else get all the glory? No way.'

She strode towards the gap in the hedgerows with her torch trained ahead of her – and the crucifix in her pocket, feeling like it was burning a hole in her gloved hand. She bent her head to duck under the overhanging branches and ventured through the rabbit hole, so to speak.

'Remember,' she recited to herself. '*Sky News Sunrise* . . . Good morning, Eamonn . . . Charlotte . . . It's Alexis here with a breaking story . . .' She picked her way through the brambles which were tearing at her clothes. 'OK, and it's over to Nazaneen with a weather update . . .'

Her torch beam picked out a deserted clearing with a muddy circle of ground surrounded by a high wall of thickets. In no way did it look inviting. It was darker than the outer reaches of space, and it smelled of death.

'Ian? You should take a look in here. It's really cool,' she lied.

Then she suddenly heard a frantic rattling of water bottles.

'Ian . . . ?' She turned the beam around to search the meadow that lay just beyond the hedgerows.

Ian wasn't there any more.

'Ian!'

She saw him stumbling away across the hillside in fear, the rucksack jangling behind him.

'You coward!' she shouted after him angrily.

'Sorry, Lex! Not worth it –' he panted over his shoulder.

'Fine!' she yelled defiantly. 'This was a once in a lifetime opportunity. And you blew it!'

She turned the torch beam back to the clearing and screamed in shock.

Something was crouched in the middle of the circle.

Before her brain could fully register what the thing was, Alexis reached for her crucifix, then fumbled and dropped the torch, her hands shaking uncontrollably. The light dropped to the ground, falling at an abject angle, leaving the clearing itself in total darkness.

She started hyperventilating, tore off one glove, pulled out her phone and started texting, desperately stabbing at the screen, her face lit up in a paroxysm of fear.

The thing came closer, avoiding the fallen torchlight so as not to be seen.

Alexis managed to hit 'Send', then turned the screen of the phone around to illuminate her attacker. Alexis recoiled in surprise, before surrendering to a full-blown, blood-curdling scream. The kind that not even the best horror films could come close to.

In less than a second, the phone was snuffed out and stamped into a hundred pieces. The crucifix fell to the ground, and Alexis was completely encompassed by the dark.

'What the hell was that . . . ?' demanded Clive from the path a few hundred metres away.

'A woman in distress,' Burke deduced.

'Oh, top marks, Ray,' Draycott snipped. 'We might have a position for you on the force.'

'I'm going in,' said Burke.

'On whose orders?' Draycott barked.

'*Hasta la vista.*' Burke lowered his night-vision goggles and set off in the direction of the scream.

'Don't be a hero!' Draycott called after him.

Another deafening howl sent birds scattering above the trees. The sound appeared to be nearer than before.

'Can we leave now?' Clive asked.

Draycott thought about it for a second. 'That's the first sensible thing you've said all day.'

Clive held up his hand in a high five. Draycott raised his hand to meet Clive's, until . . .

Clive's whole arm dropped out of reach, as his legs were pulled out from under him.

'What – ?' he yelled.

Clive hit the ground, spreadeagled and face down in the mud.

'Ouch! That reaaa-lly hurt,' he complained.

Then Clive was suddenly yanked backwards, trailing along the ground towards a large bush.

'Clive?' Draycott shouted.

'Heeeeeeelp!'

Clive clawed at the mud as he was dragged through the darkness by an unseen attacker, his legs and feet completely vanishing into the undergrowth, until only his head and the shoulders of his shell suit were visible through the bush.

'It's got my trainers off –' Clive screamed. 'I've had it! Ray?! Somebody, please!!'

Burke heard the commotion and turned his bike around.

Draycott waded in, grabbing Clive by the arms and pulling him in a desperate tug of war with the enemy. A growling, chattering noise came from the foliage.

Clive stabbed a finger at the sports bag. 'The dung! Throw the dung!'

Draycott briefly let go of Clive, who was instantly pulled even deeper into the undergrowth, until he clutched on to two hedgerows – now only the thatch of his salt-and-pepper hair was visible through the bush.

Draycott unzipped the sports bag with his free hand, turned up his nose and reached in, grabbing a handful of predator deterrent. Draycott threw it, hitting Clive squarely on the top of the head.

'Not me! The werewolf!' Clive whined.

Burke skidded to a halt, dropped his bike and grabbed Clive's arms. Clive's lower half jolted again sharply as he was pulled further backwards. Draycott threw aside the sports bag and joined Burke in holding on to Clive.

A loud ripping sound came from the undergrowth.

'It's got my trousers –' Clive screamed. 'Hurry! Please!'

Burke and Draycott dug in their heels and pulled Clive's arms. All three men screamed from the sheer exertion of it, until Clive's body was pried loose and ejected from the bushes, leaving them all in a heap. The lower half of Clive's shell suit had been torn away, leaving only a pair of red Y-fronts. The other two men did a double take.

'Well, don't just stand there – let's get out of here!' Clive shouted, pulling his jacket down, before loping towards his BMX.

'Good plan,' agreed Draycott.

'Follow me,' ordered Burke, who was still wearing the night-vision goggles.

The three of them performed a rolling start and pedalled hard downhill.

A short distance away, Ian Dulwich was still running, bottles rattling, having heard the full chorus of screams and howls from the woods. He ran down a steep path leading towards the East Heath Road entrance, then stopped, hearing a strange, whirring noise behind him.

He spun around to see two red lights flying straight towards him.

'No-no-no-no . . .' Ian stammered in terror.

He pulled his camera around to his chest and aimed the flash at the oncoming creature, pressing the button over and over again, illuminating a middle-aged man in goggles on a BMX.

Burke flinched. His infrared night-vision suddenly became a blinding snowstorm. He lifted his goggles and rubbed his eyes, steering his bike wildly off course.

Clive and Draycott followed right behind him through the darkness, exactly as they'd been instructed to.

Ian watched as the three middle-aged men on BMXs careered downhill, failed to negotiate the bend, and slammed straight into the guard rail that protected the pond.

With a deafening clang, all three men were thrown over the handlebars of their bikes and – due to the complete surprise of the impact – their bodies were so relaxed that they flew through the air with the grace of trained circus acrobats, before hitting the icy water in a hail of screams and curses.

Chapter 21
A RIDDLE WRAPPED IN A
MYSTERY, INSIDE A TEXT

That same night, Darkus digested Bogna's latest culinary offering while assembling the facts of the case – but found himself no closer to a solution. Uncle Bill had called during dinner but appeared too lovestruck to contribute anything sensible to the investigation. He'd spent the whole afternoon with Fiona Connelly and was convinced of only one thing: that she was the 'lass of his dreams'.

As Wilbur snored at his master's feet, Darkus pored over the photos he'd downloaded on to his father's computer. The images flashed by one after another: the giant paw print he'd first found on the Heath, which matched the one in Fiona's back garden; the grisly make-shift hunting lodge with its mutilated trophies hung up for the hunter to admire. But what sort of hunter had done this, and what was the motive? And how did it relate to the fact that Darkus and his dad had now been targeted by Barabas King and his pack of attack dogs?

Darkus flicked through the tortured bodies to the picture of Fiona Connelly's bed. He clicked on the screen to enlarge the image. The impressions in the mattress topper were certainly curious. Both lay curled up in foetal positions. The animal shape could have been that of a dog, a wolf, or some other creature. And the human shape was facing the animal one, in an almost protective position – although Darkus feared he was letting his imagination run away with him.

He finally flicked to the partial footprint in the bathroom, mentally noting its features, before closing the screen.

He heard Tilly making up the inflatable mattress on the landing, then he settled down on the sofa. He pulled a blanket over himself and soon fell asleep with the distant and reassuring sound of his father downstairs, talking over the case to himself, with only an occasional interruption from Bogna.

Darkus slept fitfully, seeing the phantoms of the dead pets flying through his unconscious brain; and occasionally witnessing a pair of demonic eyes watching him from deep in the woods. The woods of course were those of Hampstead Heath.

Wilbur appeared to take on Darkus's nightmares as well, and kept intermittently crying, then whimpering in his basket. Darkus comforted the dog, which also served to comfort himself, then they both returned to sleep.

But Darkus's sense of well-being didn't last long. His dreams were haunted by low, dark creatures running across the meadows and howling at the moon; then his dream-self heard a rasping gurgle, like the last breath of a dying animal, and witnessed what appeared to be blood dripping down over the skyline.

Morning arrived mercifully at 8 a.m. when Tilly burst through the door, holding a phone in her hand.

Darkus sat bolt upright, still fully clothed.

'Is it Dad?' he asked bleary-eyed. 'Is he OK?'

'Don't worry, Doc, I'm fine,' said his father, appearing in the doorway.

Wilbur roused from his slumber, looking as exhausted as his master.

'Miss Khan's on the phone,' said Tilly.

She put the call on speaker and placed it on Knightley's desk for them all to hear.

'Good morning, students,' Miss Khan's voice addressed them.

'There's no need for formality. Tell us what you've got,' requested Tilly.

'Very well,' Miss Khan began. 'This morning I received a phone call from the Headmaster about two separate incidents on Hampstead Heath last night – both relating to members of Cranston School.'

'Proceed,' said Darkus.

'Tilly, your father was involved in an ill-fated attempt to uncover the cause of the recent pet disappearances. He appears to have recruited a Chief Inspector Draycott and our PE teacher, Raymond Burke. All three men are currently recuperating at home with hypothermia, cuts and bruises.'

Tilly rolled her eyes. 'What exactly were they playing at?' she asked.

'They claim to have heard unearthly noises, and Clive believes he was attacked by a werewolf – although none of them can positively identify the assailant. Apparently, Clive was half naked when the men were rescued from the mixed bathing pond by members of the Hampstead Heath Constabulary.'

Tilly shook her head. 'Muppets.'

'In an unrelated and far more serious incident,' Miss Khan continued, 'Alexis Bateman also ventured on to the Heath last night, accompanied, somewhat reluctantly I understand, by Ian Dulwich.'

Darkus looked up. 'What did they find?'

'They also heard a howling noise, at which point Ian fled the scene,' replied Miss Khan.

'What about Alexis?' said Darkus, concerned.

'She didn't come home last night.'

Darkus rubbed the back of his head anxiously. Tilly watched his reaction closely, her brow furrowing.

'The police are conducting a search,' Miss Khan went on.

'Did Ian make a witness statement?' said Darkus.

'Yes, but he's too scared to make any sense. It was dark and he was disorientated,' replied Miss Khan. 'We do have one piece of evidence though . . .'

'Proceed,' repeated Darkus impatiently.

'Alexis's mother received a text from her at exactly eleven fifty-eight last night. It only contained three words with no punctuation, emoticons or any other clues. It simply said: *found come early*.'

'Found come early?' asked Darkus. 'All lower case?'

'Yes. Her phone was disabled, possibly destroyed, moments later.'

'Intriguing . . .' said Knightley.

'We're talking about a missing person, Dad,' snapped Darkus in uncharacteristic fashion, before steepling his fingers nervously against his forehead.

'She shouldn't have gone out there without proper back-up,' argued Tilly. 'More fool her.'

'I don't see how that's relevant now,' replied Darkus dismissively.

'A search party's combing the Heath, but it's a monumental task,' said Miss Khan.

'Found . . . come . . . early,' muttered Darkus, letting the words revolve in his mind, racking his brain for a possible meaning.

'Doc,' said his father carefully, 'if we turn this into a Missing Persons inquiry, we risk the whole investigation. There are larger powers at work here.'

'Are we concerned with saving lives? Or simply solving a case?' Darkus challenged him.

'When she wrote that article she put everyone's life at risk,' Tilly responded. 'She brought it on herself. Call it bad karma.'

Darkus frowned and stared at the carpet, searching for an answer.

Knightley approached, resting a hand on his shoulder. 'There are forces at work that mean to do us harm . . . this very night, by the light of the full moon. Alexis may have been taken for exactly that reason – to lure us out there after her. In order to get to *us*.'

'Is her life any less valuable than one of ours?' Darkus demanded.

'To be honest with you, Darkus . . . yes,' answered Tilly guiltily. 'And the dogs will be out within a matter of hours.'

'"The needs of the many outweigh the needs of the few",' quoted Knightley, although he couldn't recall exactly where he'd heard it. 'If we find whatever is perpetrating these acts, we will most probably find Alexis too. So far, our enemy has only targeted members of law enforcement. There's every reason to believe your classmate is still alive.'

'Very well,' Darkus consented, looking at Knightley then Tilly with something approaching resentment, or even contempt. 'It appears I've been outvoted,' he said and leaned towards the speakerphone. 'Please keep us posted, Miss Khan. We have a case to solve. Thank you.' He pressed a button to end the call.

Knightley and Tilly watched and waited for his next response. Wilbur whined, unsettled.

Darkus went into an almost Zen-like state of total absorption, putting every last nerve impulse in his brain to work on the problem.

After almost a minute, he said, 'Tilly . . . ?'

'Yup?'

'If I'm not mistaken, you and Alexis share the same brand of mobile phone, am I right?'

She nodded. 'Same exact one, except she's got the gold case and I like to change mine at random.'

258

'May I borrow it, please?' Darkus requested.

Tilly paused. 'Just so you know, I never let *anyone* touch my phone.' She reluctantly passed it to him.

'I promise no harm will come to it.' Then Darkus stopped, having second thoughts. 'Better yet . . . *you* be my guinea pig.'

'O – K . . .' she replied, sceptical.

Darkus passed the phone back to his stepsister, who was quite confused at this point. Knightley and Wilbur watched and waited in silence.

'OK. Ready when you are,' said Tilly.

'I'm going to ask you to compose a text message for me, but you have to write it in less than three seconds,' said Darkus, producing a stopwatch from his waistcoat pocket.

'Why?' asked Tilly.

'Just do as I say.'

'Well, who should I send it to?'

'Irrelevant. There's no need to press "Send".'

'All right,' she huffed, having no idea what this game was about.

'Are you ready?' Darkus rested his finger on the stopwatch.

Tilly poised her fingers over the touchscreen keypad. 'Shoot.'

'OK. The text message is . . . *Fiona Connelly*.'

Darkus watched the second hand start ticking. Tilly wasted a good half a second reacting to the content of the message – then quickly tapped out the words on the screen.

Darkus watched the final second elapse and clicked the stopwatch. 'Time's up!'

Tilly looked down at the screen. 'That's unbelievable.'

'What is?' asked Knightley, baffled, looking over her shoulder.

Tilly handed the phone to Knightley who examined the message window. It read: *found come early*.

'It's very simple,' explained Darkus. 'At least to a piece of word-recognition software it is,' he went on. 'Alexis was so terrified that her fingers missed some of the letters. The phone auto-corrected the letters to the most common words: *found come early*.' He concluded: 'Alexis was trying to write *Fiona Connelly*.'

'Outstanding,' said Knightley.

Tilly nodded, impressed.

Darkus put his personal feelings towards Alexis in a locked box. In order to save her he had to treat the case objectively – like any other case. He returned to his near-meditation state, talking to himself: 'We know the police are combing the Heath. There's nothing more we can do there. We know that in all likelihood they'll find nothing.

As usual, their sole purpose – along with members of the press – seems to be to corrupt the scene. Therefore, we must use the remaining daylight hours to find and follow Fiona Connelly. She's clearly protecting someone, or some*thing*. And I now believe that thing might be Barabas King.'

'Bravo,' Knightley added. 'So the two cases *are* connected?'

'We'll know for certain when the moon is up.'

'I'll stay here,' said Tilly. 'I need another few hours to finish the programming. By this evening we'll have a backdoor into Fiona's security system – which means we'll be able to watch the house ourselves, undetected.'

She looked to Darkus for approval, but received none.

'Don't mention it. Piece of cake,' she added.

But Darkus didn't even hear her, such was the intensity of his focus. He looked down to Wilbur, who watched loyally, his head still resting on the basket.

'Come on, boy. We've got work to do.'

But Wilbur didn't obey, appearing unwilling to move.

'Come on, boy,' Darkus repeated. 'What are you afraid of?'

Wilbur simply curled up more tightly in his basket and refused to budge.

'Fine,' Darkus conceded, gathering his coat and heading for the door. 'Be like that.'

Knightley nodded apprehensively to Tilly and followed his son out.

Chapter 22
THE UNLIKELY COMBINATION

Barabas King found himself in another empty building – an abandoned factory this time, chosen for its anonymity. So anonymous in fact that he didn't know where it was himself. His pack of dogs sat obediently in formation behind him, awaiting instructions.

King glanced up at the cloudy sky that was just visible through a broken skylight window. He approached a mirror, which hung over a dirty basin. He examined his face closely, looking for any telltale signs.

Then a voice appeared behind him. It was a woman, but her image was just outside the range of the reflection.

'Hello, Barabas,' she said with a clipped upper-class tone.

'I told you to stop interfering, Fiona,' King hissed.

Behind him, the dogs whined and stomped their feet, sensing something wrong.

'I can help,' she answered. 'If you'll let me.' She paused. 'Every dog can be healed. Even one as bad as you.'

'I don't need your help,' he spat. 'This is your last warning . . .'

'We'll see . . .' she said ominously. 'By the light of the moon . . .'

As her footsteps receded into the distance, the dogs began howling and barking uncontrollably.

Chapter 23
BEHAVIOURAL PROBLEMS

The Fairway cab pulled up discreetly at a street corner overlooking Hyde Park, with Knightley behind the wheel and Darkus in the back seat, each observing the scene through their own pair of binoculars.

Across the way, a film crew arrived and began setting up their equipment by a pedestrian crossing. A small throng of onlookers had gathered nearby to watch.

'Where is she . . . ?' Darkus murmured to himself.

'According to the fan website Fiona should arrive any minute,' Knightley explained. 'Tilly found that out. She's very good you know.'

'I know,' said Darkus, distracted.

A few moments later, a chauffeur-driven car parked near the crossing and Fiona Connelly stepped out, wearing a bulging raincoat, belted at the waist, a long yellow corduroy skirt and sturdy outdoor shoes. A make-up person adjusted her hair, then an assistant passed Fiona the strap of a lead, which was attached to an excitable springer spaniel.

'Heel!' Fiona instructed.

The dog stopped yapping at once and stood still.

'Goood,' she cooed.

The assembled crowd broke into light applause, after which Fiona shrugged modestly, bowed a little and waved. The Knightleys watched closely for any clue, their faces pressed against the eyecups.

The director called out instructions to the crew. 'OK, roll camera. And . . . action!'

Fiona walked along the pavement leading the springer spaniel, which was prancing at her feet. She approached the pedestrian crossing, demonstrating how to lead the dog across a busy road.

Fiona made a point of stopping at the edge of the pavement and raised her hand abruptly in an almost military salute.

'Ssssssit!'

The spaniel obeyed without question. Then Fiona extended her finger and pressed the 'Wait' button. After a few moments, the pedestrian tone started beeping and she raised the lead, signalling the dog to stand and trot across the road alongside her.

Reaching the other side, Fiona turned to the waiting camera and addressed it.

'So you see, even the cheekiest springer spaniel can be brought to heel ... with the proper discipline. So it's goodbye from me ...' She gave a gummy smile and pointed down at the spaniel. 'And it's goodbye from this *bad dog* made *good ... Good boy!*' She petted the dog vigorously.

'OK, and cut!' the director called out. 'Magic, Fifi.'

The throng of onlookers surged forward, holding out books and photos for Fiona to autograph. She gracefully signed each one, before being startled as a much larger figure bustled through the crowd towards her.

'Is that who I think it is?' said Knightley, rubbing his eyes.

'I'm afraid so,' said Darkus.

'Fifi? Ye looked pure barry out there, there's nae doubt,' said Uncle Bill, approaching her and doffing his hat.

'Monty ...' she whispered diplomatically. 'I didn't know you were coming to set?'

'Aye, I'm meeting Alan and Darkus o'er there ...'

Bill pointed directly at the cab.

'Oh great,' complained Knightley, dropping his binoculars and waving back awkwardly.

'He's a liability,' said Darkus.

Bill gave Fiona a bear hug, then excused himself and virtually skipped across the road to greet his colleagues.

'A'right, Alan? Darkus?' He attempted to lean through the cab window unsuccessfully.

'Bill, this was meant to be a surveillance operation,' Knightley explained.

'On Fifi . . . ? Why would ye wannae dae that?'

'We believe she may be in danger,' Darkus elaborated. 'From her midnight caller.'

'Nae problem, I'll park the Moby Dick outside her place and keep an eye on things, eh?'

'Using the van might be a little . . . unsubtle,' advised Knightley.

'If you agree, Dad,' began Darkus, 'I think Bill should remain as close to Fiona as possible.'

'Belter,' agreed Bill, nodding eagerly.

'Advise her that it's for her own safety. Accompany her home if necessary,' said Darkus. 'But don't let her out of your sight.'

'Beezer!' exclaimed Bill lustily, although the Knightleys had no idea what he meant.

'Be careful,' warned Darkus. 'We'll give you further instructions in a few hours.'

'Have you still got those silver bullets handy?' asked Knightley.

Bill patted his snub-nosed revolver, which was tucked in a holster under one of his generous arms. 'Dinna leave home wi'out 'em.'

'Good,' said Knightley.

Darkus glanced up at the sky, half expecting the moon

to peer back at him from behind a cloud, but it was concealing itself for as long as possible – waiting for the witching hour to arrive.

Finding their cover blown, and having to resort to leaving their prime suspect in Bill's less than capable hands, the Knightleys returned to Cherwell Place. Before they could fully unlock the door, Bogna opened it with urgent news.

'Wilbur is on strikes.'

'What d'you mean on strike?' said Knightley.

'He won't go for walk. He not eating my food,' she replied.

'Are there any *other* symptoms?' asked Knightley delicately.

'I'm home, boy,' Darkus called through the doorway.

'He acts all funny and won't leave his baskets,' explained Bogna. 'I have called Captain Reed – he's just arrived.'

Darkus led the way into the living room to find Wilbur curled up by Bogna's armchair, apparently refusing to budge. Captain Reed stood patiently by the mantel-piece, watching him.

'Darkus . . . Alan.' The captain nodded to them.

'John,' Knightley acknowledged him.

Darkus knelt by his dog, resting a protective hand on his back. 'What's wrong with him?' he asked Reed, getting straight to the point.

'Don't worry, there's nothing physically wrong with him. But he appears to be having a relapse of some kind,' Reed began. 'Possibly a touch of post-traumatic stress disorder. Brought on by what, I couldn't tell you. He's partially regressed into the fearful dog he was when you first got him.'

'I don't understand,' said Darkus.

'He's been through a lot the past seventy-two hours,' Knightley reasoned. 'We all have I suppose.'

'But I need you, Wilbur . . .' Darkus rubbed his head playfully.

The German shepherd twitched his bat-ears uncertainly. The adults looked on, concerned.

'What's wrong, boy?' Darkus whispered.

Wilbur looked up at the darkening sky outside the window, then rested his head on his paws and cried softly for a second.

Captain Reed paced by the fireplace, perplexed. 'This may sound crazy . . .'

'We don't use the c-word in this house,' Knightley pointed out.

Darkus gave his father a sceptical look.

'Well, at least, I don't,' Knightley clarified.

'But what?' Darkus asked Reed.

'He's been staring out of that window at the sky ever since I arrived. If I was a superstitious man – which I'm not – I'd say he was afraid of the full moon.'

'How could he possibly know about that?' said Darkus, petting his dog again. 'It's OK, Wilbur. There's nothing to be afraid of.'

Knightley nodded. 'It's certainly possible. The moon controls the tides, the elements, not to mention our emotions and state of mind.'

Darkus understood that the gravitational attraction of the moon affected the oceans, by causing the water to bulge, resulting in high tides – the highest one on record being over fifty metres, as he recalled, in the Bay of Fundy near Nova Scotia, Canada. However, he dismissed the moon's effect on the emotions as unscientific and impossible to prove.

Darkus got to his feet and entered the kitchen, before returning with Wilbur's beloved Metropolitan Police rubber Kong toy. 'Would this cheer you up?' he asked the mutt.

Wilbur raised his greying eyebrows.

'Tomorrow, after the full moon, we'll go to the park. Like old times.'

Wilbur suddenly rolled on to his back and wagged his tail.

'Attaboy.' Darkus broke into a smile. 'He's fine, aren't you, boy?'

Knightley and Reed exchanged a nod, appearing reassured. Bogna looked less convinced, cocked an eyebrow and returned to her duties.

Darkus went upstairs to check on Tilly's progress but found the landing and office empty, with no sign of his stepsister or her ever-present laptop computer. He checked his phone for any communication from her and, as if by magic, an email appeared:

> *Program done. Click the link below to activate it. All CCTV cameras will then switch to a pre-recorded loop, giving you freedom to move about the property. Your fingerprint will access all doors and gates. The alarm will not sound.*

Darkus smiled, wondering how and when she'd acquired his fingerprint, and admiring her devious skills. Then he read on:

> *I've gone to the Heath. It's a mystery to me but you obviously care about this girl so I'm going to find her for you. Don't try and call me – mobile signal is intermittent up here anyway. Catch you later.*
> *Xo T**

She signed off in her usual way.

Darkus's heart sank, and he immediately disobeyed her instructions and tried to call her, but it went straight to voicemail. He clicked off his phone and cursed himself for his foolish emotions, which had now put his beloved step-sister in danger – although Tilly would never tolerate him using such a term of endearment to describe her. For the first time, Darkus felt like the world was slipping out of his control and for all his careful attention to detail, the most important people in his life were now all under threat.

He glanced out of the window and calculated that there were only around three hours of daylight left. Then the Heath would be pitch dark, and the animals would come out – including the predator. Whatever it was.

Darkus realised that the time for playing his cards close to his chest was gone. He must soon disclose every-thing he knew to his father, for fear of any further repercussions. Returning downstairs, Darkus passed on Tilly's message and advised his dad that they needed to assemble the necessary equipment and set out for Hampstead Heath at once – to investigate the Connelly residence, prevent any further disappearances and hopefully draw this strange case to a close.

Chapter 24
THE TROPHY

Tilly didn't give Darkus the whole truth, nothing but the truth. She gave him enough to make him feel guilty, but not so much that it distracted him from the core of the case. She figured Darkus did the same thing to her regularly. He never gave her the full contents of his mind and frequently withheld his suspicions until he could present the solution to his eager audience on a plate.

The whole truth was that Tilly had managed to hack into Alexis's mobile phone network and – using data acquired from cellular phone masts in the area – she had triangulated the almost exact location from where Alexis's fateful last text was sent.

Using a relatively cheap handheld GPS device, Tilly followed the coordinates around the base of Parliament Hill, past various joggers and tourists, and a team of police officers picking through the undergrowth, searching for Alexis. She also overheard a handful of teenage thrill-seekers trudging through the woods, discussing the possibility of werewolves roaming the Heath, and what on earth they would do if they happened upon one.

For Tilly herself, the jury was out on the whole super-natural issue. But she'd brought a set of rosary beads that she'd inherited from her mother, just in case. They hadn't saved her mum, but maybe they would save her. She'd also brought one of Miss Khan's ultrasonic dog whistles – to cover all bases.

The path led Tilly through a gap in the undergrowth, revealing a lush meadow with a view of a spire in the distance. A fallen tree lay dramatically across one side of the meadow. Tilly checked the GPS against a detailed map of Hampstead Heath and realised she was within metres of the spot where Alexis had sent the text message.

She looked around, surveying the landscape, doing a full 360-degree scan, then stopped, seeing a small opening in the bushes directly behind her, leading into the woods. She moved closer, spotting a long, blonde hair wound around one of the thorny bushes that guarded the opening. Tilly plucked it between her fingers and held it up to the dimming light.

'I'd know that hair anywhere . . .' she whispered to herself.

Tilly rolled up her sleeves and carefully pried open the thorny gateway to the woods, revealing a lonely clearing.

It was much darker in the shadow of the forest. And colder, and scarier. Tilly felt a chill run down her spine. She observed her surroundings, finding the muddy ground was demarcated by a wall of tall thickets.

She checked her phone and found the signal bars empty.

She suddenly wondered why on earth she was doing this, especially alone. What was she trying to prove? She didn't care a hang about pushy blonde Alexis Bateman, who had quite clearly brought her fate upon herself, whatever fate it was. Was Tilly doing this in order to score points against Darkus? Or to earn his admiration and possibly martyr herself in the process?

The wind picked up, blowing the dead leaves through the air and somehow making the clearing even darker than it was already. Tilly shook her head and thought better of the whole thing.

'Forget this –' She turned around and marched towards the gap in the hedgerows, until . . .

A hoarse whisper stopped her – it was one word, spoken in a series of croaks, coming from somewhere deep in the wall of thickets. Tilly turned around and shuddered. She couldn't work out what it was, or what it was saying. It was the sound of someone who'd had the life choked out of them.

'Wa-a-aiit . . .' it said, struggling to gain volume.

Tilly bent down and approached the sound, coming face-to-face with a tall barrier of branches, vines and leaves. She ran her hand over it and realised it was a makeshift door, fabricated to look like part of the wilderness.

'Wa-a-aiiit, pleee-ase,' the voice insisted.

'Alexis?' Tilly whispered through the wall.

'Yeeee-es.'

Tilly grabbed hold of the door and pulled it to one side. A cloud of black flies swarmed out, hitting Tilly in the face and getting caught in her hair.

She screamed, swatting at them and spitting them out of her mouth, until the flies dispersed, the buzzing subsided and the full horror of the hunting lodge was revealed.

Tilly crept inside, seeing the ghoulish creatures hanging with their eye sockets gaping and their jaws yawning in pain. Tilly blocked out the nightmarish trophy gallery and focused instead on the small, still living creature huddled in the corner of the lodge.

At first, Tilly didn't even think it was Alexis. This creature was too frail and old. Her clothes were shredded, her face was drawn into itself and her once beautiful

277

blonde hair had completely faded to grey. Whatever she had witnessed had quite literally scared the life out of her – and aged her by decades.

'Hee-elp . . . me . . .' she whispered through cracked, dry lips.

'It's OK, I'm here to get you.'

Tilly checked her pulse. Alexis's heart rate was over a hundred and fifty beats per minute but she was still breathing, just about. However, her wrists and ankles were bound with thick rope, wound so tightly that it had broken the skin. The rope was looped around two massive trees to ensure there was no escape.

Tilly instantly pulled a small metal gadget from her backpack and pressed the button on the top. Alexis visibly jumped as a blade shot out of the handle. Tilly angled the flick knife on the rope around her classmate's wrist and started sawing through it. The outer strands began to fray but the rope was too thick. Tilly sawed faster, but it was no good.

Tilly checked her phone again but the signal bars were still empty. She tried to look out through the wall of thickets but the daylight was fading fast and they were too deep in the woods to cry out.

'I need to go get help,' said Tilly.

'No!' Alexis cried out. 'Don't leave me. Please-please-please-please. She's coming back . . .'

'Fiona Connelly?'

Alexis nodded quickly.

'OK, but you'll have to be patient.'

Alexis nodded and winced as Tilly angled the knife on the rope again and continued to saw.

Chapter 25
BAMPOT
(Translation: person of unsound mind)

Uncle Bill was walking on a cloud. Not only had he met the woman who might be the love of his life, but they appeared to share so many of the same interests. In the past few hours they had consumed almost a whole bottle of fine wine and three packets of chocolate digestive biscuits. Several retrievers lay prostrate around Fiona's living room. The sun was sinking in the sky, the conversation had never dried up for a moment, and he felt quite certain romance was just around the corner.

Then his secure phone rang and he glanced at the screen: *Alan Knightley*. He swiftly placed one of his exceptionally large hands over the display so as not to alert Fiona, who was sitting across from him with her legs neatly crossed.

'Sorry, Fifi . . . It's the office.'

'I understand,' she replied.

Bill glanced at his huge coat and homburg hat, which were draped over a chair nearby, and hoped he wouldn't have to put them on again quite yet – perhaps not until taking a walk of shame to his waiting Ford saloon. Casting these thoughts aside, Bill palmed the phone and raised it to his ear.

'Uncle Bill 'ere,' he grunted. 'Aye. Aye. Aye-aye . . . Aye.' He lowered the phone, looking crestfallen. 'As I suspected, Fifi. I've been called away on urgent business.'

'What a shame,' she purred. 'I thought you might stay for *dessert* . . .'

'Well, I . . .' Bill mumbled. If they'd consumed chocolate digestives for their main course, he could only imagine what she had in store for dessert.

'I was just going to pop upstairs,' she added, 'and slip into something more . . . comfortable.'

Bill's cheeks inflated involuntarily. 'Christ on a bike, zarrafakt.'

'Are you all right, Monty?'

'Nae problem, Fifi,' he said, regulating his breathing. 'One of mah men . . . is waiting . . . in a car ootside the gate. They'll make sure yoo're perfectly safe.' He scooped up his heavy coat and hat and headed for the door, feeling positively woozy.

'Wait . . .'

281

She grabbed Bill's meaty arm and drew him into a lingering kiss on the lips.

'Until we meet again,' she whispered.

'Mammy . . .' Bill wheezed.

'Sweet dreams,' she responded and sent him on his way.

'Aye.' Bill backed out of the doorway, doffing his hat and nearly tripping backwards over Fiona's Hunter boot collection. 'Cheerio for nou.' He half fell on to the gravel driveway as she closed the door behind him.

Bill straightened himself out, hoisted on his coat and hat and found himself all alone. The electric gates whirred open, ushering him out. He marched indignantly through them and scanned the street for the Ford saloon, feeling the sobering effects of the cold.

Behind him, the Knightleys emerged from the shadows, giving him a start.

'Aye mah auntie!'

'It's OK, Bill,' whispered Knightley, moving him out of sight. 'We had to get you out of there to begin the next phase of the operation.'

'What?'

'Moby Dick's parked just round the corner,' added Darkus, holding Wilbur next to him on a short lead attached to the K-9 tactical vest. 'They're watching the building.'

'What operation . . . ?' asked Bill, still trying to regain his senses.

Darkus took out his secure phone, opened the email from Tilly and tapped on the link. An activity wheel revolved on the screen, as the signal was sent.

'OK. Let's hope she doesn't disappoint,' Darkus murmured.

He glanced up at the security camera pointing down on the gate. Its red light winked once, then went black. Darkus approached the biometric fingerprint sensor by the intercom. He gently pressed his forefinger against the pad and it illuminated green. The electric gates quietly whirred open, granting them access. Darkus led Wilbur through the gates and on to the driveway.

Knightley gave Bill an earpiece and put one in his own ear also. Then he handed the Scotsman a brown paper bag filled with coffee beans.

'Would ye mind tellin' me what's going on?' Bill demanded.

'Ask *him*,' said Knightley, nodding towards his son.

'Dad and I are carrying them too,' explained Darkus. 'It's to put our opponents off the scent.'

Darkus and Wilbur led the way, taking cover behind a tree and surveying the front of the Gothic-looking house. Knightley and Bill huddled behind them. A light flicked on in a second-floor bedroom surrounded by dense ivy and wisteria branches. Fiona entered the lit bedroom and quickly closed the thin voile curtains. Her silhouette moved casually back and forth across the room.

'All right, Bill, it's simple. Don't let her out of your sight,' said Darkus. 'We'll be in radio contact at all times. If she leaves that room, you must let us know immediately.'

'I cannae see anything from doon here,' complained Bill.

'Then go a little higher,' said Darkus, pointing at a drainpipe leading straight up past the bedroom window.

'Aye, and then yer bum fell aff,' blurted Bill, indicating that he thought Darkus was joking.

'It'll give you a bird's-eye view,' agreed Knightley.

The Scotsman raised his eyebrows. 'This feels wrong,' he muttered, then ambled off towards the drainpipe. 'I could ne'er live with mah self.'

Bill grabbed hold of the drainpipe, then positioned his orthopaedic loafers on either side of it. He started breathing heavily, similar to a champion weightlifter prior to a raise. He tested his weight on the fittings, then miraculously began shuffling up the pipe at a surprising rate of speed.

The ivy and wisteria branches shook violently as he crawled up the side of the house, looking like he was threatening to pull the entire wall down.

Fiona walked to her window and peered between the curtains.

'Hold on, Bill –' Knightley whispered into his earpiece, as he and Darkus watched unseen from the shadows.

Fiona looked around, finding nothing of note, then left the window again.

'All right, Bill. Proceed,' instructed Knightley.

Bill continued his shuddering ascent, leaving a growing pile of leaves on the ground below him.

'We don't have much time,' said Darkus and led his father briskly towards the front door of the house.

Wilbur whined anxiously, sniffing the air.

Knightley stopped his son's arm. 'OK. But would you mind telling me exactly what's afoot here?'

'It's too early to say –'

'Ah-ah,' snapped Knightley. 'I think it's precisely the right time to say.'

'OK,' conceded Darkus. 'On this rare occasion, you and I are in agreement. The lunar cycle does affect the tides, the elements, possibly even people's emotions. Many things in fact. And I fear we will witness a terrifying transformation of some kind before the full moon.'

His father glanced up at the bedroom window. 'You're not telling me Fiona Connelly is a werewolf . . . ?' demanded Knightley. 'You're more certifiable than *I* am.'

But Darkus had already returned to his singular state

of mind, focusing only on the facts. 'First I need to take a closer look at the basement.'

He approached the fingerprint sensor by the front door and gently pressed his finger against the pad. Again it lit up green and the lock disengaged.

Darkus gently opened the door as Wilbur and Knightley stayed in single file behind him. The light of the doorway fanned out over a sea of sleeping dogs. Fiona's four-legged family were all stretched out on the floor, snoring.

'Remember the saying?' Darkus whispered.

'Don't worry . . . I'll let them lie,' answered Knightley, gently closing the front door behind them.

Wilbur continued sniffing the air, detecting smells that he couldn't immediately identify.

The trio crept across the entrance hall, past the slumbering canines and towards the door under the stairs that led to the basement.

Meanwhile, Bill was clambering up towards the prize, wincing as the ivy brushed against his face. A large pile of leaves and debris had collected on the ground below him, but he dared not look down for fear of losing his nerve. The light of the bedroom window shone like the pearly gates just above his head.

A spider's web stretched across his face, catching on the brim of his hat, and he shook his head violently to try to untangle himself. A large, hairy spider crossed the web, arriving at Bill's nose. Bill huffed and puffed, attempting to dislodge it, but it wouldn't move. Bill continued upwards, now drenched in sweat and with a spider on his nose, then swung his prodigious leg on to the ledge of the window, gracefully balancing himself in mid-air and allowing his right hand freedom to pinch the spider by its hind legs and cast it off into space, web and all. As Bill watched it fall, he saw the view below him, which was so far down that the perspective appeared to shift and elongate before his eyes.

Bill cursed and grabbed hold of the drainpipe with both hands, returning his attention to the window. Just at that moment, Fiona passed by the curtains, which she'd closed in a hurry a few minutes earlier, inadvertently leaving a convenient centimetre gap through which Bill could now observe her.

'OK, Alan,' he breathed into the earpiece. 'I have the birdie in mah sights.'

Fiona was relaxing in her floral wallpapered boudoir and had already removed her tweed jacket and was currently shuffling out of her tweed skirt.

'Crikey . . .' Bill murmured as the large piece of fabric flopped to the floor, along with its oversized safety pin, leaving Fiona wearing only a blouse and some very thick, winter tights.

Bill's hands went clammy and he had to wipe them one by one on the sleeves of his coat, in order to keep from sliding down the pipe. His eyes misty with perspiration, he followed orders and continued to watch.

As Darkus, Knightley and Wilbur crept down the carpeted staircase to the basement, Darkus explained himself to his dad in a whisper.

'During our site visit, several things caught my attention that I couldn't rationally explain. The sound-proofing in the basement. The reinforced glass. The two treadmills.'

Darkus held up his hand to indicate a halt, as they heard the distant whirring of machines of some kind.

They reached a white corridor that led from the stair-case to the private gym. Wilbur bobbed his snout around, sensing something, then he instantly sat down: to signal danger.

Darkus slowly moved along the corridor towards a white door with a small perspex window in it.

The mechanical whirring got louder and louder as he approached.

Knightley watched nervously as his son sidled up to the window and peered inside. Darkus spotted the source of the noise through the glass: the two treadmills were running at almost maximum speed with two fans providing air circulation. But the athletes on the running machines weren't human.

Two Rottweilers were galloping at full pelt, their muscles straining and tensing with the exertion, drool cascading and threading from their mouths. In front of the treadmills were two strings dangling from the ceiling of the gym. Both strings had objects tied to the end of them.

One of them was Darkus's lost hat.

The other was the piece of tweed from his father's jacket.

Both were hung like bait for the dogs to learn the scent. The hounds ran relentlessly towards their prey, despite not gaining any distance.

Darkus flinched, noticing the two hoodies from Victoria Station reclined on chairs behind the treadmills, both preoccupied with their smartphones. Lined up next to them were the other four Rottweilers, confined in locked cages.

Darkus turned back to his dad and used a hand signal to indicate: hostiles inside. Knightley nodded then retreated, hearing Bill's voice coming through the earpiece.

*

Three floors above, Uncle Bill had managed to wedge himself between the drainpipe and the window ledge, as if he was settling into the best seat in the house. He unconsciously reached in his coat pocket and took out a coffee bean which he popped in his mouth and bit down on with a crunch.

'She appears tae be getting undressed, Alan,' he panted into his earpiece.

Through the gap in the curtains, Fiona could be seen crossing the boudoir to sit at her dressing table with a large mirror in its centre. She sat perfectly upright and began tracing her fingers over the contours of her face, then took several cleansing wipes and began wiping away her blusher.

Strangely, she then began to speak. Uncle Bill placed his ear close to the window to try to hear exactly what she was saying, but could only make out snippets.

'Yes. Even a bad dog like *you* . . .' she appeared to say, then paused. 'Don't you take that tone with me,' she replied fiercely.

Bill adjusted his position to stare more closely through the gap and saw from the reflection in the mirror that there was *no one* else in the room. She was completely alone.

'She appears tae be talking to herself . . .' whispered Bill into the earpiece.

Fiona wagged her finger at the mirror, then stood up abruptly, causing Bill to flinch. She then crossed the room again and casually began unbuttoning her blouse.

'O-oh. The clothes are comin' aff again,' reported Bill.

Fiona left her blouse half undone and started hauling off her winter tights, hopping on one sturdy leg.

'She's takin' her tights aff . . . Aye-aye-aye . . .' Bill whispered.

Fiona stepped out of her tights, revealing two very hairy legs.

'Alan, she's . . . *hairy*,' said Bill, unsure whether this was a plus or not.

Fiona then completely removed her blouse and let it drop to the carpet . . . revealing a bizarre, padded outfit underneath with a heavy-duty zip running up from the waist to the armpit.

Bill rubbed his eyes, not quite believing what he was seeing.

'Haud on . . . She's . . .'

In one quick movement, Fiona unzipped the layer of padding and stepped clean out of the outfit to reveal an extremely hairy – and obviously *male* – torso.

Bill lurched violently, nearly falling backwards off the ledge.

'She's a *he*!'

'What?' Alan's surprise could be heard through the earpiece.

'Fiona' then removed her granny spectacles, her coloured contact lenses and her wig, then roughly tugged on her prosthetic nose, which stretched and snapped off to reveal her true, brutish face.

'She's . . .' Bill struggled to mouth the words. 'She's *Barabas King*.'

'Extraordinary,' responded Knightley.

Bill tried to breathe but found his lower lip wobbling. 'I feel verra hurt and confused right nou.'

Free from the confines of 'Fiona', Barabas puffed up his furry chest and marched back to the mirror, shouting at it so loudly that Bill nearly fell off again.

'I told you to stop interfering, Fiona!' King snarled at his reflection, then felt something in his mouth, and remembered the set of gummy dentures, which he extracted to reveal his sharpened fangs. 'You're always trying to trip me up –' King suddenly punched the mirror, shattering it to pieces. He licked the blood from his hand and pointed an accusing finger at the dressing table. '*And don't come back, ya follow me?!*'

Bill hung on to the drainpipe, his eyes wide and his cheeks palpitating.

'Alan?' he whispered desperately. 'I'm scared.'

*

Knightley responded into his earpiece from the basement. 'Darkus wants you to hold your position.'

'Aye, well, it's either tha' or fall aff,' Bill wheezed.

Knightley turned to his son, looking betrayed.

'Mind telling me how long you've known Fiona and Barabas King are the same person?'

'They're not the same person,' replied Darkus. 'They're two separate personalities inhabiting the same brain. King suffers from "split personality disorder". Fiona and King have been trying to outwit each other. One is continually trying to get rid of the other. They're at war for control of his mind.'

'How, Darkus?' his father insisted. 'How did you know?'

'The indentation on Fiona's side of the mattress topper was not consistent with a female. The contour was wrong, the shoulders were too pronounced, the hips too modest.'

'I see,' said Knightley.

'That and the partial footprint in her bathroom. It was clearly a man's foot, although she claimed not to have had any bedfellows. And the time she allegedly spent qualifying in Kenya, it coincided exactly with the years King spent in psychiatric institutions. That's where "Fiona Connelly" was created. She's the civilised side of Barabas. The side that wants to be good. An upstanding member of society. A good dog.'

'Whereas the real Barabas is bad to the bone.'

Darkus nodded. 'Fiona lives by the rule of law. Barabas lives by the law of the jungle. Which brings me to my next observation.'

'Whatever next . . .' said Knightley, caught between admiration and dread.

'The partial footprint in the bathroom shared some disturbing similarities with the paw print we found in the clearing – and in the back garden.'

'What are you saying?'

'I never said I had a complete theory,' admitted Darkus.

They were interrupted by a single bark from the gym. Followed by another and another. Suddenly, the basement erupted into a cacophony of furious barks as the two Rottweilers leaped off the treadmills and raced to the perspex window, jumping up and covering it in slobber.

'They've got the scent,' said Darkus, rummaging urgently in his jacket pocket. '*Our* scent.'

Wilbur started barking back ferociously, trying to ward them off. The hoodies could be heard shouting, trying to work out what was going on.

One of the Rottweilers reared back on its hind legs, using its front paw to depress the metal handle and open the door. Then both dogs exploded out of the gym and raced up the corridor side by side towards them, preparing to leap.

Knightley grabbed his son, ready to run, but Darkus finished inserting a pair of earplugs into Wilbur's bat-like ears, then held up the ultrasonic dog whistle and pressed the button.

The dogs appeared to freeze in mid-air, then collided with each other and fell in a heap, writhing on the floor. Upstairs, the entire family of dogs woke up, whining and crying.

In the bedroom, Barabas jolted, putting a hand to his ear in pain. He could hear the ultrasonic frequency as well. Then he whipped his hand out in rage, clearing the dressing table of its contents, sending perfume bottles, cleansers and moisturisers clattering to the floor.

Outside the bedroom window, Bill's face was just visible in the darkness, watching in terror.

Barabas spun again, tearing pictures and ornaments off the wall and leaving deep scratch marks in the floral wallpaper.

Then he turned to the window, but seemed to look straight through Bill and raised his colossal face to the sky, where, exactly on cue, the clouds parted to reveal the moon, which was full and bright.

Outside the glass, Bill watched in mute horror as King arched his back, inflated his lungs and let out an ungodly howl that threatened to shatter the windowpanes. The noise seemed to penetrate the walls of the house and ring out across the entire Heath. When King finally ran out of breath, he inhaled again, expanding his massive chest and repeating the howl once more. This time the sound was painful and tortured, as if there was yet another person – or thing – inside this man that was begging to be let out.

'Something's happening, Alan . . .' Bill whispered.

The howl juddered to a halt and King keeled over, placing his hands square on the carpet and exposing his back, which was completely matted with thick hair. In a perverse version of a yoga exercise, he raised his pelvis and extended his legs out behind him. Then he stared down at his hands, spreading his fingers and twisting his forearms with a loud clicking noise that sounded like a power tool over-tightening a nut.

Bill watched in disgust as King unnaturally rotated his wrists and lifted his hands until the thumbs dislocated themselves and bent backwards, then with a sickening series of snapping sounds, the fingers flattened, resembling a paw.

Bill started to feel his food repeating on him. The bag of coffee beans slowly emptied itself on to the ground below.

The clicking noise returned as King extended his heels until his feet appeared to fold in half and his toes lay flat on the carpet facing forward. His head then dropped between his shoulder blades and stared up at the window, lit by the full moon.

Through a process of contortion, King had, to all intents and purposes, transformed himself into a *wolf*.

Bill's white face could be seen drawing further and further away from the window, until both his hands went up into mid-air in a surrender sign and he vanished from sight – followed a moment later by a dull thud.

In the basement, Knightley tapped his earpiece. 'Bill? We thought we heard a howling noise. Bill . . . ?'

The two hoodies emerged from the gym doorway with knives in their hands. The rest of the pack yapped miserably, refusing to leave their cages. Confused, the youths picked their way over the writhing Rottweilers and marched towards Darkus and his dad with their blades extended.

'My skills aren't entirely up to this. Are yours?' enquired Knightley.

Darkus's catastrophiser whirred to life but didn't get a chance to act.

Wilbur had already run between the Knightleys and leaped at the attackers, executing a double takedown.

Wilbur bit into one attacker's arm, forcing him to drop the knife, while Darkus trod on the other one's wrist, forcing him to do the same.

'Well, that went smoothly,' said Knightley and collected their weapons, while Wilbur stood guard, growling. 'Bill, d'you read me?' he repeated into his earpiece.

Knightley was interrupted by a crash from upstairs as something smashed through a glass cabinet; then another crash that sounded like a plate glass window shattering. Darkus's catastophiser changed up a gear, the cogs spinning faster. He was painfully aware that he didn't have a complete explanation for the facts. Or for the exact nature of the transformation that had taken place above them.

Wilbur woofed and looked at the ceiling. The hoodies looked equally concerned and decided to stay on the ground for their own safety.

'It's King,' said Darkus instinctively.

Darkus led Knightley and Wilbur to the top of the staircase and opened the basement door to find a trail of destruction. Darkus took the key from the inside of the door and locked it behind him, trapping the dogs and their handlers below. Then he picked his way over the broken glass and chinaware that littered the reception rooms. One chandelier had been pulled to the ground while another hung at an indecent angle. The retrievers and lapdogs all sat cowering in silence.

Knightley grabbed his son's shoulder. 'Wait . . . Are you saying that thing we saw on the CCTV cameras was King?'

Darkus nodded. 'However improbable, it's the only explanation.'

He ran to the living-room window, just in time to see a dark shape scale the back wall and vanish over the other side.

Darkus reasoned. 'He's going to the Heath.'

Chapter 26
DOGFIGHT

Tilly sawed frantically at the last binding as the full moon rose above the trees, overlooking the clearing. Alexis watched her work, her eyes vacant and lifeless.

Tilly's attention lapsed for a second and the knife slipped, nicking Alexis's wrist, drawing blood. 'Ouch, I'm sorry –' Tilly apologised. 'I didn't hit a vein . . . I don't think.'

But Alexis didn't even seem to notice. 'Thank you for saving me, Tilly,' she whispered hoarsely.

'I haven't saved you yet,' she warned.

A quarter of a mile away, King hurdled a tree stump and galloped on all fours through the dense woods surrounding the Connelly residence. He detoured around a police search party that was still seeking Alexis Bateman, and paused on a bluff, sniffing the air to see if his enemies were in pursuit. Then he tugged on his double-jointed fingers to ensure they remained in position. The pain made him arch and howl again, his wail echoing across the Heath.

King glanced up at the moon, drawing on its immense glowing power, then scrambled up a steep incline, heading in the direction of Parliament Hill. He brushed through the middle of a pack of thrill-seekers, who took one look at the beast and fled screaming in all directions.

Wilbur led the Knightleys across the driveway snout-first, passing Bill who was sprawled on his back on the lawn.

'Bill . . .' Knightley panted. 'Are you OK? Is anything broken?'

'Verra probably,' replied Bill. 'I foresee another extended stay in the hospital. Fortuitously this pile of leaves seems tae have broken mah fall though.'

'Can you feel your toes?' said Darkus, examining Bill's orthopaedic loafers.

'Aye, Doc, most of 'em. Not tae worry. I'm just going tae have a wee rest if it's all the same tae ye.'

'I'll instruct the police to round up the dogs and seal off the area,' said Knightley.

Bill grabbed Knightley by the lapel. 'Tell Bogna I miss her.' Then he delved under his sweat-stained armpit and pulled out his revolver, offering it to him. 'I suggest ye take this . . . It's got silver bullets. I dinna know if King's a genuine werewolf, but best tae shoot first, ask questions later.'

Wilbur began bobbing his nose about to get the scent.

'We'll get you help,' Darkus assured him.

'Nae bother. Cheerio for nou,' replied Bill, defeated.

Wilbur led the Knightleys away, straining at the lead. Then the full moon appeared from behind the clouds again, painting them in blue light. The German shepherd came to a halt and cried softly.

'It's OK, boy,' whispered Darkus, then recited the K-9 promise. 'My eyes are your eyes, to watch and protect. My ears are your ears, to hear in the dark.'

Wilbur furrowed his brow, then regained the scent and led them briskly out of the gates and along the pavement towards the Heath.

'Where's he taking us?' asked Knightley between breaths.

'I think I know.'

Tilly cut through the last cord of rope and breathed a sigh of relief.

Realising she was free, Alexis struggled to her feet, shaking loose the bindings.

'OK,' whispered Tilly triumphantly. 'Let's get out of this dump.'

The two girls crawled out of the corner of the lodge, ducking low to avoid the gallery of grotesques, and crept towards the doorway, until . . .

A demonic shadow passed over the makeshift wall of branches. It was a crooked shadow of a man, bent over and distorted, walking on all fours. It was the stuff of nightmares; the manifestation of pure evil.

Tilly stopped Alexis's arm with a shaky hand. Alexis began to spiral downwards again, shaking her head back and forth in quick motions, about to scream. Tilly clamped a hand over her classmate's mouth and pulled her back into the darkness of the corner, sheltering behind the row of rotting animal carcasses.

Alexis kept shaking her head, mouthing the words silently, 'No-no-no-no . . .'

Tilly laid her back down in the position she'd been in before and arranged the ropes to look like they were intact. Alexis's eyes rolled back, barely able to stay conscious, as Tilly moved to the opposite corner, behind the body of a large dog, and froze on the spot.

Suddenly, the makeshift door was whipped open and the full horror of King appeared on all fours, backlit by the moon. He stalked into the lodge, heading for his prize, sending the trophies swinging on their hooks, casting horrific shadows that made the walls move. His jaw fell open, revealing the rows of sharpened teeth, dripping with saliva.

Alexis locked eyes with the beast and began screaming at the top of her voice, over and over again, like a horror film caught on repeat.

Tilly didn't have time to deduce who or what she was facing. She clutched her rosary beads in one hand and raised her ultrasonic device in the other.

King's head cranked round unnaturally – like a dog's – detecting her scent.

Tilly locked eyes with him. 'Chew on this . . .'

She pressed the button and the ultrasonic signal went straight through King's head, but only seemed to make him angrier.

A disjointed hand shot out and struck Tilly, violently knocking her back and sending the device tumbling to the ground, until a hind leg effortlessly stamped it to pieces.

Tilly slid backwards across the muddy floor, covering Alexis's body with her own, struggling for any kind of weapon.

King crept closer on all fours, his foul breath rising as puffs of steam from his nose and mouth. His irises expanded and contracted hungrily. He reared back on his hindquarters and prepared to strike, then a bright light flashed into his eyes, momentarily blinding him.

Tilly raised her camera-phone, firing off shot after shot. Then that too was knocked aside as King roared and raised both mangled paws.

Tilly lay back, next to Alexis, and prepared for the inevitable, until . . .

One wall of the lodge appeared to explode, as Wilbur burst through it at speed, tackling King so aggressively that they both rolled through the opposite wall and out into the moonlit clearing.

The momentum carried the two creatures several metres before they came to rest near a fallen tree.

Then the real fight began in a frenzy of biting and kicking.

Wilbur pinned King down and went straight for his sinewy neck, but King used both hands to throttle him, flipping the dog over and reversing the power balance. Wilbur yelped as he found himself pinned to the ground with King on top of him – the beast's gigantic muscles flexing and tensing. King bit the dog's ear, then Wilbur brought his hind legs through the middle of King's, and began running on the spot, battering on King's chest to give himself room to manoeuvre – his tail sweeping back and forth all the while.

Darkus and his dad stumbled through the opening in the undergrowth and beheld the spectacle.

'Wilbur!' Darkus cried out.

But Wilbur ignored his master, wrestling with King as the beast held him in a death-grip.

Tilly and Alexis crawled out of the collapsed remains of the lodge, shaking and covered in animal blood, then ran to Knightley who immediately took off his coat and sheltered them.

King and Wilbur rolled over each other again, crossing half of the clearing in a single fluid motion. King landed up on top again, striking downwards and tearing at Wilbur's chest, shredding the tactical vest. Wilbur struggled, snarling and biting into thin air.

'Dad!!' Darkus cried out. 'Do something!'

Knightley pulled out his ultrasonic device, but Darkus stopped his hand.

'No – it'll affect Wilbur more than him.'

Knightley reached in his other pocket and pulled out Uncle Bill's revolver, then aimed it at the two grappling opponents. Knightley squinted down the barrel of the gun, positioning the bead on King.

At that moment, the two creatures rolled again, in a chaotic mess of cries and kicking limbs. King still remained on top, pinning Wilbur down and biting down on his neck. Knightley re-trained the revolver, lowering his brow, deepening his gaze and steadying his breathing.

Darkus shook his head, not wanting to watch – but realised there was no other way. 'Do it. Pull the trigger.'

King reared up, ready to deliver the death blow when –

Knightley fired the gun, striking King cleanly in the shoulder and propelling him off Wilbur and on to the ground.

Knightley sighed with relief, before King roared and struggled to his feet again, flexing his massive torso. Knightley raised the barrel again and fired, striking King in the thigh.

King floundered on all fours, disoriented, then took off galloping through the gap in the woods.

Darkus ran to Wilbur's side, collapsing in the mud next to him where the dog was panting and heaving. Darkus began to check him over as Knightley, Tilly and Alexis remained huddled, watching in silence.

King climbed Parliament Hill for what he knew would be the last time. He was losing blood rapidly and he was too far from home, and in fact didn't really know where home was any more. He just knew he wanted to see the city one more time. He loped to the summit of the hill and saw the London skyline twinkling, stretched out below him in all its majesty, with the perfect full moon shining overhead.

As his chest heaved and fell, his jaw dropped at the sheer magic of it all.

Several hundred metres below, concealed in dense trees, the long barrel of a silenced sniper's rifle also observed the moment.

An infrared sight lined up King in the cross hairs, accompanied by the clipped tone of a professional marksman.

'Mr Underwood? I have the shot.'

A faltering man's voice responded from behind him. 'He's a l-liability.' Then he completed the instruction: 'Put him down.'

The silenced bullet hit home with a thud.

King never knew what hit him, and collapsed to the ground in a lifeless heap. The city lights, and the full moon, bore silent witness. The newspapers would report that the body of crime boss Barabas King was found stripped naked in a suspected gangland hit. The coroner's report would find that although King was double-jointed and able to dislocate limbs at will – not to mention being extremely hairy – he was, without a shadow of a doubt, *human*.

*

308

In the clearing, Darkus leaned over Wilbur, balancing the dog's head in his arms. Wilbur raised his eyebrows expectantly and twitched his whiskers.

'Hold on, boy, you're going to be OK,' Darkus whispered, then Wilbur rolled over, revealing a deep gash in his chest.

Darkus touched it, then took his fingers away, wet with blood. Wilbur panted faster.

'Dad? Get help!' Darkus commanded, then turned back to Wilbur, fighting back tears. 'My eyes are your eyes, to watch and protect . . . My ears are your ears, to hear in the dark . . . And my life is yours, as long as you live . . .'

Chapter 27
WILBUR

Darkus watched as the shaggy tail bobbed and weaved playfully through the tall grass, like a periscope. Hampstead Heath looked less sinister by daylight and the recent storms had washed away the few remaining 'lost' posters.

Darkus sat back on the bench and watched the ducks take off and land on the glittering surface of the ponds. Then they all appeared to take flight at once, as a voice interrupted him.

'Doc?'

His father stood on the path, having approached unnoticed.

'Your mother's worried about you,' said Knightley, then paused, hoping for a response. 'So's Tilly. And Alexis. I knew where to find you,' he added.

Darkus didn't turn round, but could now see the Fairway cab out of the corner of his eye, stationed in the car park with Bogna standing guard in front of it.

'I told you. I'm not interested in talking to you,' said Darkus.

Knightley crept forward slowly and sat down on the bench next to him.

The dog's tail zigzagged happily further away across the meadow.

Darkus budged over on the wooden seat to create distance from his dad. Behind him, on the slats of the bench, was an engraving.

My eyes are your eyes . . .
For my beloved Wilbur, February 4ᵗʰ 2014

The shaggy tail finally emerged from the tall grass to reveal a Labrador retriever, which ran back to the side of another young master, who ruffled the mutt's hair as it jumped up on his chest. Darkus watched as the boy and his dog walked off into the distance.

'I'm so, so sorry, Darkus,' his father whispered.

Darkus continued staring ahead, then reached in his jacket pocket and pulled out the stainless-steel card holder – and handed it back to his dad. Knightley cracked it open to see the *Knightley & Son* business cards, still inside.

'I'm leaving the business,' Darkus said simply.

'It's not that simple . . . The Combination –'

'Until you can be an ordinary dad, and I can be an ordinary son, there's nothing to talk about.' Darkus looked back at the engraving. 'You see, if we were ordinary . . . he'd still be here.'

Knightley's eyes misted up and he adjusted his hat, looking down.

Darkus got to his feet, buttoned up his nylon anorak and walked along the pathway in the opposite direction to his dad.

Knightley took a few moments to compose himself, then stood up too.

'Doc, wait – !'

But the words evaporated in the wintery air, because the path was empty. And his son was already long gone.

WILL RETURN . . .

Find out more at:
www.knightleyandson.com

ROHAN GAVIN

is an author and screenwriter based in London.
His enduring love of detective fiction,
dogs and digestives inspired him to
write this book, the second in a series.